Also by Jim Gullo

Just Let Me Play: The Story of Charlie Sifford

Seattle & Portland for Dummies

The Insider's Guide to Seattle & Portland

The Importance of Hilary Rodham Clinton

A Traveler's Guide to the Plantation South

Fountain of Youth

Trading Manny: How a Father & Son Learned to

Love Baseball Again

GROUCH BAG

A NOVEL

BY JIM GULLO

J. [signature]

Hooray, hooray, hooray

YAM HILL PUBLISHING

BROOKLYN • PARIS • MCMINNVILLE

Grouch Bag, a novel. Copyright ©2016 by Jim Gullo.

This book is a work of historical fiction, and any similarities to real persons, living or deceased, are purely coincidental.

For Sam Gladstein, and a lifetime of love and laughter.
We will eat all the sandwiches, always.

"Outside of a dog, a book is man's best friend. Inside of a
dog, it's too dark to read."

-- *Groucho Marx*

CHAPTER ONE: PROPER PUNCTUATION

"What's so funny, Mr. Markowitz?" Mr. Yanuzzi demanded, breaking into my happy, private place. "Does this amuse you? Is my office a source of great amusement for you? Aren't you ever serious?"

I was in trouble. Again. He was right that I'm never serious. I just can't help it that I'm funny. It's the tragic reality of being the Class Clown of Patton Middle School.

I shook my head no, coughed into my fist and looked around to admire the décor of my Assistant Principal's dungeon lair . . . I mean office at Patton, where I am a seventh-grader and a regular visitor, for disciplinary reasons largely beyond my control, to Mr. Yanuzzi's basement of horror. He had made some changes since my last visit.

"I like what you did with the place," I said in a feeble attempt to butter him up. I pointed to the west wall. "Very inspiring."

Three of the walls were plain, drab cinderblocks painted in a color that surely must have been called Dismal Lifeless Gray in the paint catalogue.

They were bare, but on the fourth wall he had mounted a collection of historical artifacts that were once used by Assistant Principals to torture and otherwise impart "important life lessons," as he put it, to innocent schoolchildren. These included a bullwhip and a wooden cricket bat that they used back in the day to respectively whip and paddle children into sobbing submission; a hickory switch, which is like a thin branch of wood from a tree that makes an impressive whipping noise when waved sharply through the air, the better to tear at terrified and tender young flesh; and an old wooden ruler that looks like it was hewn out of the trunk of an oak tree and must weigh about fifteen pounds.

"Why the ruler?" I wanted to add, "Is it to measure your victims before you torture them?" but kept my pie-hole shut for a change.

"I'm glad you asked, Mr. Markowitz," he said, carefully removing the ruler from its moorings.

He stroked it gently, like it was a kitten or similar soft creature, and then suddenly whacked it sharply on the side of his desk, which made a violent, brittle sound that echoed off the walls of his office and seemed to linger in the air. The sharp noise made me jump about two feet up off my chair and then settle back down onto it with a hard thump. "We assistant principals once used these rulers to rap on the knuckles of, if you'll excuse the expression, unruly children."

"Good one, Mr. Y," I said. "Ruler. Unruly children. I'll have to remember that."

"Very painful in its day," he said wistfully as he replaced the ruler on the wall. "Very effective. The children shaped up fast after the ruler treatment. AFTER THE PAIN SUBSIDED!" he practically shouted, shoving his face so close to mine that I could practically see and smell the garlic oozing out of the pores on his nose.

I ignored the smell and pressed on with my buttering-up. "Hey, cool. What's with the Cat in the Hat lid?" I pointed to a long, cone-shaped hat, also mounted on the wall. Round at the bottom, narrowing to a point at the top, red and white stripes. It didn't look particularly terrifying or pain-inflicting.

He gazed at the hat with what I can only describe as sheer contentment. "Ah, you mean the dunce cap," he said. "In the old days, before there were laws and community standards about shaming children, we would make a bad child sit in a corner and wear this hat. "

He sighed, as if recalling happier days. "Do you know what a dunce is, Markowitz?" He looked around as if to make sure that nobody was listening, and then whispered, "Well it's the stupidest person in the world.

"When you wore this hat, the other children would jeer and point at you and tell you that you're stupid. 'Look at the dunce! Tommy's the dunce! Tommy's so stupid!'" He shook his head as if remembering old times. "You've never known shame until you've been forced to wear the dunce cap."

(It is only in the spirit of total disclosure that I point out that Mr. Yanuzzi's first name is Thomas. I'm quite sure there is no connection.)

He lovingly rubbed his fingers on the cap. "Indescribable humiliation," he added. To himself, he muttered, "Can't hit the children. Can't call them stupid anymore. Can't humiliate them. Their mommies will call the principal and the school board."

Mr. Yanuzzi, I noticed, mutters a lot. More than the average grown-up, I mean.

He returned the hat to the wall and turned back to me. "Class clowns lost their senses of humor quickly after a cap treatment. Lean closer, Mr. Markowitz," he concluded. "Put your ear to the wall and maybe you can hear the screams of the children who have come before you.

"Children who couldn't get serious."

I did as I was told. The wall was cold to my ear. It sounded like . . . a cold wall.

My best friend Omar has an expression for that dreadful room deep in the bowels of our school. Omar says it's the place where all laughter goes to die.

And Class Clowns, too. Which pretty much describes me. I've been called a lot of things and, unfortunately, Class Clown is the one that sticks. There is even a picture of me in the yearbook with a caption that pins that title on me and seals my fate: Josh Markowitz, Class Clown.

Oh, yeah, that's me. Keeper of the Comedy. Jail-Keeper of the Jokes. Or as Omar sometimes refers to me, "The Humor." As in, "Somebody call The Humor and tell him to meet us downtown."

Well, it beats being named Class Mime.

Or Most Likely to Grow Hair From the Nostrils and Become a Terrorist.

Or Class Malpractice Attorney.

There was the long answer and the short answer for why I had been sent to the AP's office on this fine morning. The long answer had a good deal to do with Elizabeth Walcot Woolcott smiling at me and saying hello. That had never happened before. She was wearing the black-framed glasses with the silver chain that allowed them to hang from her neck, and her long, black hair was tied up in a neat, prim bun on the back of her head. Every time I see her these days I get a little stupid – forgetting my name, forgetting how to walk without stumbling, stuff like that.

Elizabeth was a bit complicated, because she was really two people. On most days, she was plain old Amy Connors, who was born and raised in

McMinnville and to my knowledge has never set foot outside of Yamhill County. We have known each other since we were in pre-school. But then about six months ago, at the start of the seventh grade, Amy started pretending to be an English exchange student named Elizabeth Walcot Woolcott who had come to live with the Connors family.

"I'm from the Kensington neighborhood of London, you know. It's where the posh people live," she announced in a perfect Princess Kate accent.

Amy/Elizabeth used the word posh about thirty times an hour when she was the English exchange student. She could take a good four minutes saying her made-up name.

"No, it's Waaalllcooooott. Elizabeth Waaalllcooooott Wooooollllcooooooott. Rather posh name, don't you think?"

She was so good at dressing, talking and acting the part that half the teachers really thought they were instructing a proper young lady from the United Kingdom. Why she would do this was anybody's guess. In her own way, Amy/Elizabeth was just funny like that, I suppose.

On other days, when the glasses were pink or red, and the black hair hung down past her shoulders, Amy didn't bother with the English act. She was just Amy Connors, but she would ask if anyone had seen her English cousin Lizzie – "From across the pond, you know?" -- around that week.

And she would never, ever break character and let on that she was kidding, which I like enormously.

I liked Amy okay, but, weirdly, I found myself looking forward to seeing Elizabeth. Rather attracted to her poshness, you might say. Until today, she had completely ignored me, and when she finally did look my way, I naturally got into trouble.

The long answer for Mr. Yanuzzi, continued, was that Elizabeth Walcot Woolcott had sidled up to me on the way into Language Arts and whispered, "Hello, Josh."

Which she pronounced Jawsh, like Jaws. "I'm having a dickens of a time with the homework."

When she said the word "homework" it was if all time stood still, and a melody of vowel sounds previously unheard in Oregon spewed from the angelic harp of her pretty, red mouth.

"Heeeyaaoooommme. Wook."

"The what?" I asked, just to get her to say it again.

"You know, the heh-oooooo-mmmmm-wooooook."

I was instantly rendered speechless, and followed her into class like a little, lost lamb.

I couldn't quite put this all into words for Mr. Yanuzzi, so I stuck to the short answer for why I had been sent there. Which was that Mr. Brewer, the regular LA teacher, was out sick, and Mrs. Koberlein, who was so nervous and skittish that she may have been descended from cats, asked the class for a sentence to punctuate. And for whatever reason, for this is the cruel fate of Class Clowns, I was struck by a pretty funny idea. So I raised my hand.

So did Stevie SanPedro, who hates me with a cold, lingering fury – hates me like he hates liver and onions, or getting x-rays at the dentist, or being chosen last for dodgeball, which always happens because he's been known to turn on his own teammates and fling balls at them. Stevie SanPedro is not exactly what you would call a real team player.

He raised his hand and waved it like he was in a boat that had been lost at sea for a month and a plane was flying overhead. When Mrs. Koberlein called on me instead of him, Stevie flung down his hand, shot me a look packed with razor blades and cat vomit, and loudly said, "Aw, crap!"

The sentence I offered was, OMAR SAID THE TEACHER IS STUPID.

Everyone started laughing, Omar leaned over from his desk and punched me on the arm, and then Mrs. Koberlein in turn punched my ticket for a one-way ride to the Assistant Principal's chamber of horrors. Do not pass Go, do not collect two hundred dollars, do not beat yourself with a hickory switch.

I didn't even have time to add the proper punctuation: "OMAR," SAID THE TEACHER, "IS STUPID."

It was worth it, because as I was leaving the classroom, Amy Connors – I mean Elizabeth Walcot Woolcott -- leaned over and whispered, "Bloody good show, Jawsh. Well done."

Score one for the clown boy. I grinned all the way to the basement, and right up to the point when Mr. Yanuzzi barked, "Wipe that smile off your face," and I pulled out a Handi-Wipe that I had been saving for just that occasion and did as I was told.

My grin was barely wiped off when he grabbed the handy towelette from my hand and shoved it into the garbage can.

"See," I said to Mr. Y., "Mrs. Koberlein just misunderstood. And proper punctuation would have cleared everything up.

"Mr. Yanuzzi," I declared, slapping the top of his desk for emphasis, "I am all about proper punctuation."

Mr. Yanuzzi looked down at the floor and shook his head slowly from side to side. He made a fist out of his left hand and rubbed it with his right hand as he silently shook his head. Then he furiously whipped the hickory switch through the air a half-dozen times. It made a sound like cartoon characters make when they've been run through with a buzz saw or barbed wire and fall to the ground in sections.

"Where does it start?" he muttered.

"Excuse me?"

"This comedy. Always telling jokes. Always trying to be funny. Where does it start?"

I shook my head. "I'm not sure that it either starts or ends, sir."

He frowned. "No," he said slowly, "it has to start somewhere. And one of these days, I'd like to find out where."

His mouth then contorted into what can only be described as an evil grin. "And oh yes, it definitely ends, Markowitz. It ends right here, in this room." He whipped the hickory switch through the air again, and then said the words that I've always dreaded.

"Four days detention."

"But that's not fair," I yelped.

"Make it five, then," he said with another evil grin. "How you like me now?"

"But I'll miss baseball!" We had a big game coming up, and if I didn't practice, I wouldn't play.

He ignored me. "That's the price you pay for being such a funny guy. Now get out, Mr. Markowitz. And don't let me see you in here again. Or there will be big trouble. And pain inflicted. Your detention begins this afternoon."

Lash my back with forty strokes of the bullwhip. Rap the ruler across my knuckles until they bleed. Make me sit in the middle of Main Street wearing a stupid, pointy dunce cap. Anything but detention.

I slunk out of there in a bad mood. A beaten man. A victim of my joke-telling talent. A martyr to the cause of entertainment and laughter.

I slunk that way all the way to my locker, slunking down the A Hall, slunking past the Commons, head down, a living embodiment of the word, "mope."

But when I opened my locker, something fell out that brought me right out of my funk, or slunk. Popping out and landing at my feet was a pair of those novelty glasses that you see at the Dollar Store, with fake eyebrows and a big nose and moustache attached.

Groucho Glasses, they're called.

I knew that from watching old movies with my grandfather, who always kept a pair handy and liked to watch old comedies while wearing them. Why? you ask. Because my grandfather is completely goofy, that's why. The glasses, I learned as a very young child, mimicked the makeup and glasses worn by an old comedian named Groucho Marx who made a bunch of funny movies with his brothers about 800 years ago.

It got even weirder. Attached to the glasses was a card that read, SLIVERS'S MAGIC TRICKS. PRACTICAL JOKES, CLOWNING. THE SOURCE OF ALL HUMOR. On the back of the card was scrawled the words that would forever change my life: "I can get you out of detention. Come to my shop tonight at 6. And kid...come alone."

I drew in a sharp breath and looked around to see if Omar was playing some kind of hideous trick on me. There was nobody in the hall. I looked at the card again. The address was in a bad part of town that I'm not supposed to visit on my own. I ran my finger along the fake glasses, the eyebrows, the nose and moustache, and then put the glasses into my pocket.

The bell rang, causing me to jump. I quickly closed my locker and took stock of the situation.

A fake English girl was approaching fast from the starboard side. Her name was Elizabeth Walcot Woolcott and she was way posh. I had a sudden, overwhelming desire to ask her to go out with me, but for some reason my tongue had swollen to the size of a tennis ball in my mouth and the only words I could get out sounded like a parched man who had just walked across the entire Kalahari Desert begging for a drink of water. "Ah…um…[hideous gargling sound in back of throat]…well…"

Farther down the hall, a serious dork was glaring at me. Stevie San Pedro slammed his locker and gave me an evil eye.

According to the note attached to the Groucho glasses, there was a slim chance that I could get out of detention, but I had no idea who or what Slivers was. Put another way, a stranger had left me a note and a cheesy gift of fake glasses and asked me to come to the creepiest part of town just as it was getting dark. What could possibly go wrong?

That, my friend, might just be the understatement of the century. Or rather, of the last 104 years, as I was about to find out.

CHAPTER TWO: POSH

Amy Connors…I mean, Elizabeth Walcot Woolcott walked up to me, holding her biology book in front of her with both hands. She was wearing a plaid skirt, knee socks, a blouse and a vest onto which were pinned about 15 buttons depicting the Tower of London.

"Walk with me, Jawsh?" she said.

I nodded stupidly, still rendered mute, and fell into step beside her. It was downright weird that I didn't have the slightest hesitation to talk with Amy Connors, but with Elizabeth W.W. I became a massive idiot. I feared that I might never be able to speak again, but it didn't seem to matter, as she did all of the talking.

"Amy and I? We are actually fourth cousins," Elizabeth Walcot Woolcott began in her posh British accent. "Actually" started with a sound that was more like the "o" in "octet" than the "a" in "apple." Cousins came out like *cozzens*. *Where octually fawth cozzens.*

The empty hallway had suddenly erupted into astonishing life, like an artery that is switched back on after a bypass operation. The huge eighth-graders lumbered down the center, the puny sixth-graders stuck to the edges, and lovers who hadn't seen each other for as much as two entire periods clung together like starfish by the water fountains.

"Identical cousins, *octually*," she continued, smoothing the skirt with a brush of her hand. "You'll find that we laugh alike, we walk alike…"

"Sometimes you even talk alike," I quickly said.

"Oh, rather," she said with a short giggle. Some people make jokes. Amy/Elizabeth lives in one. As a self-appointed Class Clown, I kind of admire that.

"Indeed. Two of a kind, *octually*," she added. "Well, must totter off. Auntie's likely to have some biscuits waiting at home. And crisps."

"Or cookies and potato chips," I said. "That's what we call them here, in America."

"Indeed? Must make a note of that. Learning the old local lingo, you know, and all that rot."

She was two steps in front of me and getting away when I somehow summoned more courage than I have ever had, combined, in my twelve years. "Amy? I mean, Elizabeth?" I called out.

She turned and faced me. "Yes, Jawsh?"

"Um, tomorrow night, as you know, is the first night of spring break. Are you going on vacation?"

"Do you mean on holiday? No. Auntie will be ringing up the governess, and Uncle spends most of his time on the loo."

"Well, I don't know what any of that means. But would you like to meet me downtown at Serendipity for an ice-cream? Around seven o'clock? My treat."

Elizabeth/Amy smiled and did a cute thing where she rose up on her toes and then back down again. "I should be delighted, Jawsh," she said.

I was confused. "You should be, or you are?"

"It means the same thing in England."

I grinned, too, and felt a surge of incredible, instant relief flush through me. "Then it's a date," I said.

"Oh, I say. It rather is. Toodle-oo, Jawsh." And she turned and walked away, and skipped a couple of times, too. When she opened the door and stepped outside, she broke into a run.

I felt great for about five seconds, until Stevie SanPedro came up behind me and shoved me. "Nice joke in class, Marko-worst," he sneered. "Too bad you got detention. Hope you won't miss any baseball practice because of it."

Stevie thought he was a better second baseman than me. He thought he was the next Robinson Cano.

But actually he was more like Robinson Cannot.

"Hey Stevie," I said, "What's an invisible gas that you can smell like a mile away and makes people vomit and have convulsions?"

He looked at me suspiciously. "I don't know. What?"

"You."

Stevie slunk away like the beaten, miserable mongrel dog that he is. I made a left and went to detention. Have I mentioned how much I hate detention?

CHAPTER THREE: FROM THE DIARY OF ELIZABETH WALCOT WOOLCOTT

Cousin Amy is off playing field hockey or lacrosse or something equally and positively – no, EPICALLY -- beastly, so I am taking this time to have a nice spot of tea and record a few thoughts in my secret journal, which I have entitled I LOVE YOU PRINCE HARRY. I am using the teapot with the tea cozy that Nanny knitted for me when I was barely out of the pram. The tea is English Breakfast because they haven't yet invented English Afternoon. I would positively kill for a scone with clotted cream and a dollop of apricot jam, but we must make do here in the colonies and suffer hardships in the name of cultural exchange.

First, diary, Josh Markowitz is GORGEOUS. And so clever. Today he made positively the most fab joke about punctuation that I'm quite sure has ever been told. At least on this side of the pond. In my native Kensington, which is positively the most posh part of London (as you, diary, well know), the lads are all so droll that they make excellent jokes about punctuation before they've even finished their kippers and porridge for breakfast.

But we're not in Kensington anymore, are we? We're living in a fairly dreary little town in Oregon, aren't we? Where nothing ever happens, does it? And they've never even heard of having exchange students, much less meeting one who is very proper and posh. Good gosh, half of the kids thought that an exchange student was a girl who wanted to use the boy's loo. Well, bollocks to that – I will bring them some cultural awareness if it kills me.

So we will keep our upper lips stiff and just bear up, won't we? Because we (and I am using the royal "we" here) are strong English women and we're made of stern stuff.

Worst thing that happened today: That dreadful Steven SanPedro slipped me a note in math class, and when I opened it, it said, "I know you're really Amy." What a twit. Everyone knows that she's my cousin and that we are vastly, VASTLY different. For one thing, Amy is a girl and I am a lady. Amy is plain and I am posh. I hereby resolve that we shall never open another note from him.

I second the resolution. All in favor?
Resolution passed.

Best thing that happened today: Josh Markowitz asked me out for an ice-cream, or "glace" as our French friends across the Channel would call it. I immediately accepted. I shall wear my finest jumper and most sensible *shoes, because maybe Josh will want to go on a long walk, too, for which I would be most delighted. Maybe, too, he'll want to discuss word choices and imagery in the second through fifth Harry Potters, and ask me to recite a brief biography of J.K. Rowling's early career.*

Oh diary, can't a girl dream anymore?

Must dash. Downton Abbey is starting soon. I shall kiss my secret poster of Prince Harry and say "ta" for now.

Yours very truly, Elizabeth Wulcot Woolcott. That's Waaallllcotttt. Wallllcottt Woooollllcottttt. From the Kensington neighborhood of London, of course, which is quite posh.

CHAPTER FOUR: I MUST BE GOING

I have lived in McMinnville all my life and had never even heard of Slivers' Magic Shop. It was in a part of town that was all warehouses and next to the railroad tracks, where you could reliably encounter heavily tattooed men named Skin who wander up and down the sidings muttering complaints about the government. I wasn't supposed to go there alone.

But I'll do just about anything to get out of detention. I was pretty nervous when I crossed over Fourth Street on my bike and was about to enter the warehouse district, but then all of my jitters disappeared when I heard the familiar sound of a bike riding just behind me that had the unmistakable sound of gears rattling.

A voice behind me called out, "I didn't do it."

To which I immediately replied, "That's what she said."

That was the standard greeting of catch-phrases between me and my pal Omar, and I have to say that I've never been happier to see his goofy, asymmetrical face and hair that sticks out in every direction, like a terrified crowd rushing for the exits of a movie theater that is on fire.

I pulled my bike over to the side of the road and stopped and he glided to a stop beside me. He was wearing his standard outfit of ratty, old sweat pants with patches on the knees that his Mom had ironed on, and a stained gray hoodie over a Charlie Brown, striped t-shirt that was two sizes too small. Omar's family didn't have any money and he liked to say that his wardrobe was carefully selected from clothes on the lowest bargain rack of Goodwill. Sometimes he had to wear three pairs of pants at once because they were all so full of holes that it took three pairs to give him full leg and booty coverage.

It didn't really matter to Omar, because he wore thick glasses and was practically blind without them, and social nuances like wearing matching clothes in correct sizes were lost on him.

"Hello, I must be going," he said. Another standard greeting between us. "Where you headed?"

So I filled him in on how I had gotten detention, and how I was headed to the magic shop to get bailed out. With any luck, this guy Slivers could fix it so I might be able to return to baseball practice the next day. I reached into my pocket to show him the Groucho glasses that had been left for me, and when I did, I felt the twenty-dollar bill that my Mom had given me that morning for spring break allowance and general, all-around good behavior. I felt guilty because although Omar never,

ever asks me for money, I knew that the twenty could buy him and his three brothers and sisters enough lunch money to last them two weeks.

Omar whistled. "That's rough. You should have just told Yanuzzi the funniest joke ever written."

In unison, we both said, in German accents, "Two peanuts were walking down zee road. One was assaulted. A…salted…peanut."

My dad had told us that one. He said that during World War II the Germans had engaged their most brilliant scientists to create a joke that would bring the Allies to their knees, and after months of brainstorming, that corny peanut joke was the best they could do.

Instead, as it turned out, it was the best my dad could do.

Omar and I liked the same funny stuff. Everything from Adam Sandler movies, Kevin Hart and the Jimmys, Fallon and Kimmel, to humor that goes way back, like The Simpsons. If there is one quality that I'd ever want in a best friend, it is that we could laugh together, and that is why Omar and I have been as tight as twins since we first met and started making up knock-knock jokes on the spot.

I told Omar about Slivers, and how he told me to be at the shop at six o'clock sharp. "And look what he left behind," I said, pulling out the plastic eyeglasses with attached nose and moustache.

"What are those?"

"Groucho glasses," I said. "Haven't you ever heard of Groucho glasses?"

"Uh...no."

These days you could ask most kids if they know who the Marx brothers are, and they'll think you're talking about some guys who make basketball dunking videos on YouTube. I only knew about them because of my crazy grandfather and the old, black-and-white Marx Brothers movies he made me watch: *Horsefeathers, Animal Crackers, Duck Soup*. The Marxes – Groucho, Harpo and Chico were not only their stage names, but the names that they used in real life -- were just about the funniest, most irreverent comics ever during their run from the 1920s through the '40s. They had all passed away to that great comedy graveyard long before I was even born.

"Never mind, I'll tell you about them later."

I looked at my watch. Two minutes to six. "Shoot, I've got to get going," I told Omar. He started to ride with me, but then I remembered something. "He told me that I have to come alone."

Omar frowned and reached into his pocket. He pulled out a shiny new quarter and handed it to me. Omar was always doing stuff like that, handing out his last nickel, or in this case, quarter. I took the coin, knowing that I'd find a way to get it back to him down the road. "Never let this out of your sight," he said, trying to sound serious and failing miserably.

"I'll always keep it close to my heart," I said, putting it in my back pocket.

He laughed and waved, and that was the last I saw of Omar for about a hundred years.

CHAPTER FIVE: THE GREAT WANDINI

At the warehouse, a very old man opened the door and beckoned me inside. I fought back an urge to turn and run. "Hurry, hurry, we mustn't be late," said Slivers. It took me about three seconds to realize that there was something, I don't know, *off* about him.

For one thing, his hair was purple and stood out on either side of his ears in tufts. He was also shorter than a sixth grader but looked to be, like, seventy years old. He wore a ragged old suit jacket over an oversized bright green tie over a plaid shirt, a bowler hat and what can only be described as clown shoes. The man wore shoes that were five sizes too big and turned up at the toe.

There is no delicate way to put this, so I'll just say it: The old man was a clown. And I don't mean that he dressed in a clownish fashion. He really was a clown.

What was my final clue? In addition to his purple hair and plaid jacket and tie, he had attached a green, sponge clown's nose to his nose, and he had smeared circles of white makeup on his wrinkled cheeks, while his eyes were surrounded by diamonds of more makeup.

Do I know a clown when I see one, or what?

"Sounds like you're in a world of trouble, kid," he said, nodding his head in the general direction of Patton Middle School. "I think I can help you out."

I looked at the ground, shook my head and kicked some dirt with the toe of my shoe. "Thanks, Mister," I said, "but nobody can help me."

His eyes bored right into me. "Sure I can help. I can get you out of that detention. And you can help me. I heard that you're a pretty funny guy, and I need a funny guy for a little job."

"What kind of job?"

"We must hurry." He beckoned me towards the back of the shop, and then stopped to admire my fake nose and eyeglasses, which I had pulled out of my pocket to show him.

"Are these yours?" I asked.

"Ah!" was his only answer, "I see that you favor the Marxes."

I handed the glasses to him and he carefully fingered the plastic frame and ran his thumb along the moustache. "I sold the first pair of these sixty years ago," he murmured. "Groucho thought they were the dumbest thing he'd ever seen. 'Slivers,' he said, 'I'll be a monkey's uncle if you sell even a dozen pairs of these.' When we sold the hundred-thousandth pair in 1973, I sent him a crate of bananas."

I had no idea what he was talking about. He dropped the glasses on the floor and was suddenly walking again, faster than I expected.

"You knew the Marx Brothers?" I shouted at his retreating back.

He just waved his hand, beckoning me to catch up.

I hurried to catch up to Slivers, who was somehow now way ahead of me and nearly to the back of the store. It was way creepy back there. The dust was so thick that it had collected a layer of dust. There were dismembered body parts of mannequins lying on the shelves. At least I hoped they were mannequins. It wasn't really a magic store at all, but kind of a warehouse full of old stuff – posters of magicians, and trick lamps that puffed out smoke, old books covered in dust, decks of marked cards, and those ancient machines that you put a penny into and crank a handle that makes a bunch of cards with drawings on them spin around and look like animation. The stuff was piled up on long wooden racks and dusty tables, with no apparent order or design to any of it.

"Late for what?" I asked, catching my breath. "See, all I wanted was to maybe buy something funny. Give it to my teacher to get out of detention."

He stopped me with an impatient wave of his hand. "You can't buy the heart and soul of comedy," he said. "You have to feel it in here!" He reached into his suit jacket and pulled out a large, red, heart-shaped box wrapped with a red ribbon, like you get for Valentine's chocolates. He waved the box at me and then threw it aside. "In fact, most comedians say it finds you, not the other way around."

He whirled around to face me. It was surprising that he could suddenly move so quickly. "But sometimes, comedy doesn't quite find you when it should and we have to give it a little boost. That's why I brought you here, son. Or should I say, Class Clown?"

"How did you know that about me?"

"Never mind that!" He clapped his hands together and held them in front of his chest. "What a bright young man! And you favor the Marxes, am I correct?" He reached into another pocket of his suit jacket and pulled out a brass horn with a big black bulb on the end. Slivers squeezed the black bulb twice: HONK HONK. "That's good, because they need your help. There is hardly a moment to lose. We are so close to losing the Marx Brothers forever."

I was probably the only kid in town that understood what he meant with the horn bit. The honking taxi horn was a big part of Harpo Marx's act. He always played a mute in the movies, and always had a horn to honk. Slivers honked one more time and then tossed the horn aside.

"The Marx Brothers need your help!" he repeated. "A hundred and four years ago – this very instant, in fact -- they weren't sure if they should be singers or comics. You have to set them on the right path!"

I didn't get this at all. "A hundred and four years ago? But they were famous comedians way before I was even born. Heck, they were all dead and gone before my grandfather ever showed me their movies."

Slivers nodded. "Ah, but sometimes things aren't what they seem. Tell me what would have happened if they never got a start in comedy." As he waited for me to answer, he leaned back against a shelf and drummed his fingers impatiently, glanced at his watch, did a big double-take as if the watch was alive, blew on it, held it up to his ear and shook it, crossed his arms, looked up at the ceiling and pretended to whistle.

Just another clown doing an "I'm waiting" routine.

"Um…they never would have made any movies?"

"Good guess!" he shouted. "And the world would have been deprived of a great deal of laughter. Our lives would all be much sadder." He made a big, exaggerated sad face, as only clowns can do.

"That's why we need comedy keepers, kid. To get the laughter started. After that it has a life of its own. Let me show you something, Josh."

"You know my name?"

"I know everything," he said over his shoulder, waving a hand in the air. "I'm 147 years old!" He shuffled over to a corner of the shop where, under a lamp, what looked like the front page of an old newspaper had been laid on top of a table. Except this newspaper was made out of metal, and I could see that every letter of every headline and story was composed of a single bit of metal with that letter stamped into it. I had heard about this once in a class, that in the old days, before everything went digital, newspapers were assembled by hand like this by people called typesetters. They would assemble each story letter by letter and then the big metal plate would go to the printing press to be printed onto newsprint.

The newspaper in front of us was dated 1908 and was from New York City. He jabbed a finger at the bottom right of the page. The headline said,

"Vaudevillians Set for Trial," and the first line of the story said, "Four brothers named Marx who have performed together as a vaudeville singing act will go to trial for robbery, fraud and conspiracy next month..." The story ended there.

"But that's ridiculous," I said. "Everybody knows their movies." Well, everybody except nine-tenths of the kids who live in McMinnville.

"Nope," said Slivers. "Without a boost from the future, they never had a chance to start. Nobody encouraged them to take up comedy. They never made a single movie or told a single joke. Without help from the future, they were nothing. They were just four extremely funny brothers who never went anywhere. Where do you think comedy comes from, Josh?"

I did my best expression of a slack-jawed idiot. I had no answer.

He leaned in closer to me and his voice dropped to a whisper. "It comes from right here," he said, jabbing me in the chest with his finger. "At this very moment in time, in fact, the great Marx Brothers aren't sure what or who they are. It's 1908, and they're stuck. They think they're singers, or they might even quit show business altogether. Maybe even turn to a life of crime." He poked an old, scrawny finger at the newspaper headline and raised his fake eyebrows at me. "That's where you come in."

"Excuse me?"

He cupped his hands over his mouth and practically shouted, "I said, 'That's where you come in.'" He dropped his hands and said in a normal voice, "Do you know how they say that every creative person, especially comics, needs inspiration? Well, you're going to inspire the Marx Brothers. They need you right this minute, there's no time to lose. Convince them that their destiny lies in being funny. And then I'll get you out of detention."

I pointed to the newspaper. "But that story isn't finished. It just trails off."

And then Slivers did something that made the tiny hairs on the back of my neck stand straight up and do a 21-gun salute. He waved his hand over the metal newspaper, and when I looked again the headline had changed. "Marx Brothers Newest Film a Laugh-Riot Smash!" it exclaimed. The story began, "With 'A Day at the Races,' the Brothers Marx reaffirm that they are about the funniest thing going this side of greased piglets."

The date of the newspaper had changed, too. It was now 1937. But then Slivers waved his hand again and the story vanished. It went back to the 1908 dateline and the headline about the brothers going to jail.

"Cool," was about the best I could muster. At the moment, I mean.

Okay. Slivers the clown was not only old, and a dreadful dresser. He was nuts. Crackers. Bat-poop crazy. Screws loose . . . toys in the attic . . . crazy.

"And how do you suppose I'm going to accomplish this?" I politely asked, because I find it helpful to use my best manners when I'm alone in a dark warehouse downtown with a complete and utter mental case. I looked around to see if there were any exits, trapdoors or windows I could jump out of.

"Behold, my young friend, The Great Wandini!" With a great flourish, like a magician would do, he waved his arm to the side and stepped aside to reveal one of those dumb old fortune-telling machines sitting on the shelf behind him. It was so old and dusty that it looked like it had been sitting there untouched for a hundred years.

The Great Wandini consisted of a glass case with the head of a dummy inside that had been painted and decorated to look like a magician, with a faded, chipped purple turban on the head and glass eyes that were green and blue. Outside of the glass box was a wooden lever in the shape of a hand mounted on a stick that you were supposed to grasp with your hand while you made a wish. It had probably once been painted white, but was so worn and faded that it was now kind of yellow and bare wood. Underneath the hand, painted in what had probably once been bright colors, was the inscription, "The Great Wandini! Ask Him Anything and Your Wishes Will Come True!"

Slivers' voice was like a carnival barker, as if he were summoning a crowd to his tent at a country fair. By the faraway look in his eyes, I got the feeling that Slivers was imagining himself to also be far, far away, in another place and time. Maybe the dawn of time. The thought was yet another thing to give me the creeps. He waved his arm again with another grand flourish.

"Ask The Great Wandini and he will answer your darkest, deepest questions!"

I shrugged my shoulders. "Uh, Great Wandini..." I began.

Slivers interrupted me with a loud stage whisper. "Kid, you have to hold his hand when you ask."

And then the weirdest thing happened. When I stepped forward and put my hand around the faded, old wooden hand of The Great Wandini, the box with the magician's head inside suddenly lit up. Which nearly made me jump a foot from surprise. But I held onto the hand.

"Ask him. Hurry," whispered Slivers again.

I cleared my throat. "Oh great Wandini," I began, getting into the spirit of things, "please summon all of your great wisdom."

Slivers clapped his hands together, delighted.

I looked at him and grinned. This was kind of fun, if utterly dorky. "Summon your wisdom," I continued, "and tell me, oh Great Wandini, what is the heart and soul of real comedy? And I don't just mean cheap laughs, like Stevie San Pedro gets when he pulls Ruben Dong's shorts down in gym class in front of girls. I mean real comedy."

Slivers's hands were still held together in front of him. He had a huge, expectant smile on his face.

Nothing happened. Pretty much like I thought it wouldn't.

Still holding the wooden hand, I turned my head to face Slivers and watched as the smile on his face drained away into a puzzled frown. "Why isn't it working?" he mumbled to himself.

Because it's stupid? I wanted to say, but didn't. Because it's like, a hundred years old and people don't believe in magic fortune tellers in wood and glass boxes anymore? Because it's getting late and my mom is going to murder me for being downtown after dark, even if the zombies at the back of your warehouse don't murder me first? But I was too polite to say any of those things, so I just shrugged my shoulders and said, "Beats me."

Slivers's face lit up and he pointed his index finger straight up. "Ah! I forgot," he exclaimed. "The magic token! I always forget the magic token."

"Magic token?" I said. "I don't know what you mean..."

He reached into yet another pocket of his coat and came out with a little, brass-colored coin, about the size of a quarter, that had an M stamped out of the middle of it.

Check that. I turned it upside down. It was a W. For the Great Wandini.

"It doesn't work without the magic token!" Slivers exclaimed. "Why, that would be ridiculous!"

Slivers reached over to the side of the Great Wandini box, and his wrinkled fingers found a slot back there, kind of hidden by the wooden molding that ran around the box. I heard the token go in and clink and rattle.

And then the Great Wandini got even nuttier. Colored lights began to flash on the inside of the glass box, and I swear I could see life come into the eyes of the wooden magician's head inside. A flicker of something that was like recognition, where before there had only been dull glass eyes. Something else occurred to me at that moment, and I looked even harder at the magician. I'm darned if he didn't look exactly like Vice-President Joe Biden. In a turban.

But before I could really register it, all of a sudden Slivers's hand was tightening like a vise on my arm. He pulled on me to get my attention away from the box, and then his wrinkled, painted old face was right in my grill and he was staring into my eyes.

"Now listen to me, this is important," he said sharply. "Are you listening?" He pulled something else out from inside his coat, a long funnel-shaped thing that he stuck in his ear. Ear horns were what deaf people used to have a hundred years ago to try to hear. You stuck the small part in your ear and pointed the big end at the person talking to try to amplify the sound.

I have no idea why I know that.

Then he threw it aside.

Suddenly, there was a loud noise coming from everywhere, a noise that seemed to be made up of a hundred different sounds at once. It grew and grew in intensity. I had to lean closer to Slivers to hear him.

"You have one week to get this done, and then you must come back. And watch out for the cops, they'll be looking for you."

"Looking for me? Why? And what happens if I don't come back in a week? And Slivers," I shouted, because the noise around us had gotten even louder, "where the heck am I going? How do I even get back?"

He grinned. "Simple," he said. "Text me."

Slivers stepped back quickly. "Have a nice trip, and give my regards to Frenchie and Minnie." And then he bowed. Just before everything went white, he held up his hand to show me something. He was holding my phone, which he had just slipped out of my pocket. In its place I felt something small and round – another magic token.

"How am I supposed to text you if you have my phone?" I shouted.

He just grinned a big, stupid, clown grin, raised his index finger as if he had just been struck with a sudden inspiration, and then poked himself in the eye and fell over backwards.

That was the last thing I saw before everything went white.

The white light that I saw seemed to come from Joe Biden's . . . I mean the magician's . . . head, inside that glass box, a light so bright and intense that I couldn't see anything for a minute. The cacophony of noise got even louder. It reached a crescendo of sound that was so loud and close that it was like a train was bearing down on me.

I blinked, the light faded, and then I suddenly wasn't in Slivers's Magic Shop anymore, and it wasn't night time in McMinnville. I was standing on a street.

In a strange city. In broad daylight.

And, in fact, a train WAS bearing down on me.

A streetcar train, its bells clanging, was just a few feet away from me and closing fast. And there was nothing I could do to avoid being hit by it.

CHAPTER SIX: CALL ME JULIUS

I instinctively closed my eyes and braced myself for the impact. Then I felt the hit, but it came from the wrong direction and was a lot softer than being hit by a train. I found myself lying on the street, knocked flat and with the wind half- knocked out of me, but happily alive. Somebody had sent me flying, tackling me from behind, out of the way of the streetcar. And without a second to spare. I rolled over in time to see the streetcar, just inches away from where I lay on the street, rolling noisily away from me, its passengers not even noticing that I had nearly been cut in half by it.

Note to Slivers: You might want to check street traffic before you put somebody down in time in the middle of a busy boulevard.

I slowly gathered myself and turned around to a sitting position. A young man was peering down at me. He was wearing clothes that looked like they were from a very old movie – knickers and a white shirt and a kind of overcoat made out of a stiff, gray fabric, and shoes of a very stiff, brown leather. At his throat was a wide bow tie, and on his head he wore an old, gray derby hat that was covered in dust.

"You okay, kid?" he asked. "You must not be from Brooklyn if you can't dodge streetcars any better than that. You just about got knocked back into the nineteenth century by the Lexington Avenue number 402. I'd personally rather be run over by the Broadway/7th Avenue line. It's fancy schmancy. Only the better classes of people get run over by that train. And speaking of fancy, get a load of those duds you're wearing. Where you from, kid, some kind of circus?"

I rubbed my eyes and tried to gather my wits. I brushed off my hoodie and jeans. "Lexington Avenue?" I croaked. "Broadway? Am I in New York City or something?"

He looked at me curiously. "Well, your guess is as good as mine," said the young man. "Say, call me Julius," he said, offering his hand to me and pulling me up to my feet. "Or call me Harriet. Personally, I don't care what you call me, just as long as you don't call me late for supper."

I took a deep breath and blew it out slowly. Every part of me seemed to be unbroken and intact. Except for the small fact that I wondered if I was losing my mind. Everything around me was different and unfamiliar. "I'm Josh. Josh Markowitz," I said. "Thank you for saving me from that, um, streetcar. I must have not been paying attention."

"You're welcome, Josh Markowitz. Why, with a moniker like that you must have all of the girls falling for you back in Ireland, huh?"

I grinned and shook my head. "Not Ireland," I said. "More like McMinnville, Oregon."

His eyebrows shot up, and he took his hat off and held it over his heart. He raised the other hand up like he was about to make a great speech. The other people on the street ignored him and brushed past us, as if they were in a great hurry to get somewhere. "A country boy!" he exclaimed. "Up at the crack of dawn! Milking the chickens and gathering eggs from the cows! Churning the cream into…"

He hesitated and looked back at me. I was smiling from his impromptu little street performance. "Uh, kid, what exactly do you churn cream into?" he asked in a loud stage whisper.

"Beats me," I said.

"Well, have it your way," he said, replacing the hat back onto his head. "As for me, if it doesn't come from the Second Avenue Delicatessen, I don't wanna know where it came from."

I looked around to take stock of my surroundings. It looked like a big city, alright, with tall buildings and stores and lots of people milling around. But there were hardly any cars on the street, and the ones that were there were super old, like the original Ford Model T's. There were more horses on the street, many of them pulling buggies, than there were cars. There were tons of people out, and they were all dressed in old-fashioned clothes, the men in the same dark suit and hat that Julius was wearing. The ladies wore hats and long, flowing dresses, and most of them carried umbrellas, even though it wasn't raining.

The din of sound was the same as what I heard at Slivers's shop, but now I could sort it out a little: Streetcar bells ringing and people yelling and vendors hawking fish and vegetables and kids shouting to each other. Across the street from us was a nice park that had a sign by it that said Union Square. The whole thing looked, felt and even smelled different than anything I had ever experienced.

"Let me get this straight," I said slowly. "I'm in New York City, right?"

Julius again looked at me like I had just fallen from a space ship. Or in my case, a time warp. "You bet your life you are," he said.

I looked around again. "Just for the sake of curiosity...what year is it?"

He frowned and inspected my face with his eyes again. "Well what year do you think it is, kid?" he snapped. "It's 1908, of course, and if I have any say in it, it will continue to be right up until 1909. Say, you must have taken a knock to the head when you danced the tango with that streetcar. You'd better come home with me and let Frenchie and Minnie have a look at you."

He suddenly adopted the stance of a dancer and twirled around me with his imaginary partner. Then he said, to the imaginary partner, "Darling, you dance divinely. Do you tango often? See you at the next ball?" He made a little two-finger wave and said "Bye bye, don't be a stranger" before returning his attention to me.

Frenchie and Minnie? They were the people that Slivers said I should say hello to. And I had no idea who they were.

"Sure," I said. "I guess. Say, maybe you can help me out. I'm looking for the Marx Brothers. Groucho and Harpo and Chico and Gummo and Zeppo. They're comedians. You ever heard of them? They must be doing a performance or something this week. Where's the nearest comedy club?"

He stopped in his tracks and looked at me curiously. "The Marx Brothers, you say? You're looking for some Marx Brothers who are comics? Well, it's a big city, kid. Never heard of them in my life. For that matter, I've never heard of a comedy club, either. Oregon must be a very funny place, judging from the likes of you. But then, I haven't heard of a lot of people. And I aim to keep it that way. You coming?"

When he turned on his heel and began walking away from me, he did it with an odd, funny, kind of careening walk, bent over at the waist and darting ahead with long, exaggerated strides, his right hand held to his hip. After we walked a block, he stopped and faced me.

"Groucho, you say?" he asked. "You're looking for someone named Groucho?"

"Yep. Groucho Marx."

He shook his head. "Doesn't ring a bell. Doesn't even ring a bathtub. And believe you me, I've seen some bathtub rings that would make your head spin. Why, my Uncle Al Shean once made a bathtub ring like Alexander Graham Bell's first telephone. Now follow me close, kid. We're heading up to East Ninety-Third Street, and in that neighborhood a guy like you can find real trouble. And if you don't have time for real trouble we'll find you some fake trouble. We'd better get that head of yours looked at, and after that I'm going to have my own head examined."

He turned again and darted up the street with his funny walk. Looking both ways for any streetcars or horse-drawn carriages that wished to cut me in half, I crossed the street and followed him.

CHAPTER SEVEN: FROM THE DIARY OF AMY CONNORS

Wow, diary, I haven't seen Cousin Lizzie from the Kensington neighborhood of London so upset since Zack Geary asked her if she was Irish and did she know how to riverdance. I'm guessing she had a date with Josh M. last night, and I'm pretty sure that he totally stood her up.

Like, totally . . . stood . . . her . . . up.

I only know this because six kids from school saw her waiting for an hour outside of Serendipity, looking miserable standing there with her dumb umbrella, which she calls a bumbershoot. Stupid boys in cars yelled things at her like did she want to see their fish and chips. Janice B. and Grace R. were nice and offered to buy her an ice-cream. But she just said no, you're AWFULLY kind to ask, and then she started crying and ran away from them.

I just know this because they told me later on the phone. It's not like I was there or anything. I was busy all night watching videos of screaming goats.

She must have walked around town by herself for a good two hours, I'm guessing, because she didn't get home until late, and then went straight to her room. After that, all I heard were things being thrown around and the word 'bloody" yelled about ten thousand times. "Bloody boys!" "Bloody heck!" "Bloody Josh bloody Markowitz!" It was like a vampire movie in there, or a new episode of the Walking Dead, with all of the bloodies.

I feel kind of bad, diary. I should have gone with her and tried to protect her. I'm really surprised that Josh did that, offered to take her out for ice-cream on the first night of spring break and then totally forgot to show up, or even call us. I mean, call Lizzie and cancel the date. I mean, he could have called me, too, and explained what happened and I would have told Lizzie. It's not like I've waited by the phone all day for him to call. Stupid phone that never rings anymore, and would it have killed him to ring us up and explain?

I mean, I've known Josh all my life, ever since Care For Kids daycare and the time we exchanged diapers when we were, like, three. I've never known him to lie or not do something that he says he's going to do. Even though he's the Class Clown he's generally a pretty straight-up guy.

Until now. Now he's the meanest, lowest snake in Patton Middle School, and he will pay for this. You mess with Elizabeth Walcot Woolcott, you're messing with me.

Well, it's his loss. Lizzie's a great girl, and very posh, which I guess means cool and stylish in some kind of English way, since she says it so often. I know for a fact that Stevie San Pedro has been barking up her tree, so maybe she'll go out with him instead. And then the next time either Lizzie or I see Josh, we can laugh in his face and say, "Ha ha ha. The LOL's on you. Don't text us, we'll text you."

Well, diary, at least now I have something to do during spring break. I'm going to devote this time to finding out where Josh Markowitz was last night. And who he was with. And then I will make him pay. It's the least I can do for my cousin from across the pond. She hasn't come out of her room all day, and all she wanted for breakfast was something called a rasher of bacon, which mum, I mean Mom, brought her.

Nobody treats my girl, Elizabeth Walcot Woolcott, that way.

And by nobody I mean no boy. Ever. I'm going to go tell Lizzie right now that nobody is just the same as no boy without the "d," which stands for damned, which is what Josh Markowitz is going to be once I get my hands on him.

You will pay for this, Josh Markowitz, and now you've got two girls mad at you. And one of them doesn't have English manners or politeness, and is quite willing to slap the excuse-me out of you and call you out in front of the whole school.

I mentioned this to Omar, btw, about Josh not showing up, and he kind of went white and started stammering that he didn't know where Josh was, but there must be a really good reason why Josh stood me, he meant Lizzie, up. And then he suddenly jumped on his bike and started pedaling really fast towards downtown McMinnville. Said he had to go see a clown.

As if! What's with these boys and their crazy stories? Has the whole world gone totally nutball?

Boys. Lizzie says they're so much more civilized in England or Great Britain or the United Kingdom. Whichever one she's from, and I don't know why it's so "Great" if the pies there are mostly filled with meat and mashed potatoes. Yuck.

CHAPTER EIGHT: THE BELLBOY

"Say, do you follow baseball?" Julius asked me. He had been walking so fast, in that funny, careening walk of his, that I nearly had to run to keep up with him. It was hot outside, I bet over eighty degrees and humid, and I welcomed the break when we paused on the corner of Broadway and East Twenty-Ninth Street. Across the street was one of the most beautiful and ornate buildings I have ever seen, with a sign in gold lettering that said it was the Seville Hotel.

"I love baseball," I said. "I play second base on my team back home."

"An infielder, huh? You must have some pretty good wheels, and a good pair of hands. Maybe later we'll go up the hill and see Cobb play. Best ballplayer ever, and yes, I have seen the great Christy Mathewson and the not-so-great Bonehead Merkle."

Cobb? TY Cobb? I tried hard to remember my baseball history – he had been a great outfielder for the Detroit Tigers, I think, a long, long time ago. But now that long time ago was the present for me, a present that I barely recalled from my history classes and the books about baseball! that my dad halfheartedly read to me. Like my grandfather, if it wasn't about comedy, Dad wasn't really into it.

"So Detroit is in town?" I said, trying hard to sound casual and like I knew what I was talking about. "Are they playing against the Yankees? And Babe Ruth?"

Julius drew himself up and puffed out his chest in an exaggerated way, like he had been insulted. "Yankees?" he nearly shouted. "Yankees? Why, suh, I'll have you know that I'm a southern gentleman, and there will be no talk of Yankees here on my plantation! And I don't know about this Ruth to whom you refer, suh, but down South we don't cotton to having women on our baseball teams. Or babies, either."

He changed back to his normal voice. "You got the Detroit part right, kid, but I don't know what you mean about the Yankees. Those Tigers have their hands full with the Highlanders." He again looked at me curiously, his eyes boring into me as if he were trying to figure something out about me. "You're really not from around here, are you?"

I vaguely recalled that the New York Yankees were originally called the Highlanders, because their first ballpark was built on a hilly area in northern Manhattan. Beats me about the Babe Ruth part. Maybe he really was still a baby in 1908. "No, like I said, I'm…"

"From Oregon," he said, raising his eyebrows and nodding his head in a big, exaggerated way, as if he knew that I was trying to cover something up. "Sure you are, kid. And I'm on loan from the King of Siam." He reached into his pocket and pulled out a cigar, which he stuck into his mouth without lighting it.

He pointed to the Seville Hotel across the street. "Feast your eyes on that, Josh," he said. "Finest hotel in the world since it went up six years ago. And if they keep hiring idiots to work there, it might last another six months before it goes right back down again. See what I mean?"

He pointed to the front of the hotel. At first all I saw was an elegant woman, all dressed up in a fancy dress and hat and high heels, walking a little poodle dog on a leash past the main entrance. But then I saw that right behind her was a bellboy from the hotel, dressed in a bright, ornate uniform of dark blue pants with a velvet stripe down the leg, a purple uniform coat with two rows of brass buttons down the front, white gloves and a bright red pillbox hat that stayed on his head by means of a thick, braided cord that went under his chin.

As I watched, I saw that the bellboy was making fun of the lady, following her and pretending to walk his own imaginary dog on a pretend leash. He held his nose up in the air like he was the snootiest person in the world and sashayed along, just like the woman was walking. It was a totally great impersonation of the lady's walk, and suddenly the bellboy had an audience. People on the sidewalk had stopped what they were doing and were watching him and laughing, but the woman who was walking the dog was oblivious to him. When she noticed that something was going on, she looked back, and with perfect timing he immediately stopped his prancing and pretended to water the flowers at the front of the hotel. The second that she turned away from him, he started mimicking her again, and the people watching roared with laughter.

Julius sighed and glanced at his watch. "I'll give him about thirty more seconds. And then he'll be looking for a new job again."

The bellboy then walked up to a man who was standing on the sidewalk reading a newspaper. The man looked wealthy and important in an expensive, dark suit, patent leather shoes and a round, black stovepipe hat like the kind Abraham Lincoln wore. The bellboy walked right up to the man, stood beside him and pretended to start reading his own paper, busily turning the pages, checking an imaginary watch and acting like he was the most important person in the world. His caricature of the wealthy businessman was dead-on perfect.

The man turned to say something to him, which I'm pretty sure was the 1908 equivalent of "Go take a hike," and the bellboy did the funniest thing I ever saw. Grinning at the man, he raised his leg up from the knee and bumped it on the side of the man, and then grabbed the man's arm so that his hand held the bellboy's leg. The bellboy just stood there grinning as the man held his leg until he realized what he was doing and quickly pulled his hand away.

Julius shook his head. "He never tires of that leg gag. Watch."

Then the bellboy did it AGAIN...raised his leg up against the man's side and nudged the man's arm to make him hold the leg. The businessman pulled his hand away in disgust. Then he raised a finger and started to shake it in the face of the bellboy, obviously telling him off. The bellboy nodded and grinned as if he were listening carefully. And then he calmly reached over, took the man's top hat off his head and took a big bite out of the rim before carefully putting it back on the guy's noggin. He then started to pull strips from the man's newspaper and eat them, too. The man finally threw the rest of the paper to the ground and stalked off, furious.

Well, the crowd that had stopped to watch was just about rolling on the ground in laughter at that point, and so was I. I couldn't believe my eyes at the way the bellboy had played that dude.

Julius, who was also grinning in spite of himself, looked down at his watch and said, "Here comes the seven twenty-five, right on schedule."

Sure enough, another bellman emerged from the hotel, this one older and obviously in charge, and began waving his arms and screaming at the young bellboy, who then proceeded to take off his uniform, starting with the hat and continuing with the ornate jacket, the gloves and the pants, right there on the sidewalk, and throw each piece to the ground in mock rage until he was standing there in his underwear. He managed to do the whole thing without saying a word or even making a sound.

Julius tapped me on the arm and we walked across the street, just as the older bellman shouted, "You're fired! And don't come back!"

We walked up to the bellboy in his underwear, who was grinning and obviously pleased with himself. "You finished? Or shall we wait for the encore," asked Julius.

"Yeah, I'm done," said the bellboy. "Who's your friend?"

Julius turned to me. "Josh," he said with a sigh, "I'd like you to meet my unemployed brother. Adolph, meet Josh. He's from Oregon. First time he's ever been to New York City. Or so he says."

Adolph turned to me and grinned and stuck out a hand. "Pleased to meet you, Josh," he said. "I wish I could tell you that there will be another show at eight, but I'm afraid I'm done here." He turned to Julius and jerked his head in the direction of the hotel. "Couldn't stand it another minute," he said. "Bunch of stuffed shirts in there. Who needs it?"

His voice was gentle and kind, and I instantly put two and two together. This guy Adolph was a terrific mime and clown. And although he wasn't wearing his trademark wig or hobo suit, he had those Marx Brothers eyes and nose. He and Julius almost looked like twins, their features were so similar. And to top it all off, he was flat-out crazy, and willing to do anything for a laugh. I looked from one brother to the other. Julius had the same eyes and nose, and by the way he talked and the funny walk he did, well, the conclusion was so obvious that I couldn't believe I hadn't figured it out before.

"You're Harpo Marx," I blurted out to Adolph. "And you must be Groucho!"

Both brothers looked at me curiously. "Who?" they both asked.

"Harpo Marx. The greatest clown and mime the world has ever known! And Groucho Marx, one of the funniest comedians of the 20th century. Um," I said, quickly doing the math in my head, "this is the 20th century, isn't it?"

Adolph was smiling at me, but his face had a quizzical expression. "How did you know that I play the harp, Josh?" he asked. "I've never done that in public. Nobody knows about it. And who's Harpo?"

They exchanged a look that suggested that I was flat out nuts. And then I remembered what Slivers had said: "They don't know that they're comedians yet. You've got to help them." Just my luck, Slivers had sent me back in time too early, and instead of meeting Groucho and Harpo, I had crossed paths with two guys named Julius and Adolph Marx.

"I just mean that you played that lady and the rich businessman beautifully," I blurted out. "Like you were playing a musical instrument or something."

Then I tried to change the subject. "Is there a place around here that we can get a drink? I'm dying of thirst. And I'll buy."

"Hang on a second, Josh," said Adolph. "I can't walk all the way home in my underwear." He ran inside the hotel and came out a minute later, holding a fistful of clothes as the head bellman and the hotel manager yelled at him from the door and shook their fists. He laughed as he slid into his shirt and pants, tied his bow tie and put a heavy, long formal coat over everything. He stuck out his tongue and made a face at them and then fell into place with us on the sidewalk as we walked uptown.

"So, Josh from Oregon, what's it going to be?" asked Julius. "Beer? Whiskey? You look a little young to be a drinking man."

I grinned. "I just meant something cold and wet. Where can we get a Coke around here?"

The two Marx brothers exchanged an anxious look. "You want to drink coal?" asked Adolph. "Are you feeling okay, kid?"

Darn it! I'm pretty sure that Coca-Cola had been invented in the South by 1908, but I guess it still hadn't made its way to New York. Once again I had shown that I was way out of place...or in my case, way out of time.

"Um…silly me," I said. I laced my fingers together, put them under my chin and did a silly little swooning dance. Exactly as Groucho did in the movies that I had seen.

Julius laughed. Adolph did too. "You know, I like this kid," said Adolph.

"Yeah?" said Julius. "Well I like a good story. And I've got a sneaking feeling that Josh from Oregon has one to tell.

"You know what else I like?" he said. He stopped in the middle of the street, reached one hand up towards the sky and made a pose like a great actor on stage, not caring at all about all of the people around us who swerved out of our way. "The theater!" he yelled.

Adolph stopped and did the same thing, reaching up one hand and yelling, "The theater!"

So I did it, too, right there on a dirt-paved street. With the Marx Brothers. In 1908.

They laughed and put their arms around me, and we continued walking together uptown. And for a few minutes there, I thought that being the Class Clown of Patton Middle School and getting to meet two of my comic idols was the best possible thing that could ever happen to a person. Ever.

I would change my mind about that soon, of course.

CHAPTER NINE: MULCAHY

"He took a bump to the head," Julius explained to Adolph. "I was taking him uptown to Frenchie and Minnie so they could take a gander at him."

"Oh, they'll fix you up in no time," said Adolph. He stopped at some steps that led to an underground store. "They might not have any coal to drink, but we can get a phosphate in here."

He steered us into a dark little shop where a man behind the counter was wearing an all-white outfit and white hat. On the counter were three big glass jars full of what looked to be juice, with limes, peaches and cherries floating in them. "Three cherry phosphates, and make it snappy," Julius said to him. "And if you can't make it snappy, then make it quick. And if you're out of quick then I'll take three straws. Stop me if I'm going too fast for you."

The man shook his head, bewildered at this rapid-fire delivery. I could see that Julius was just getting started and was about to go into one of his routines. But then suddenly a policeman walked in and both of the Marx brothers got very quiet. He was a big, strong man, over six feet tall and two hundred pounds, and he wore a blue uniform, with a tall, round hat like a helmet and a walrus moustache.

The policeman was carrying a heavy nightstick in one hand. He eyed the brothers suspiciously, and then cast a long, questioning look at me, running his eyes up and down my clothes.

"You boys aren't from around here, are yas?" he asked. He had an Irish accent that made the word "boys" sound like "buys," and "aren't" sounded like "air-unt." He had an Irish name, too, sewn onto his shirt: Mulcahy.

The two Marx brothers looked straight ahead, not making eye contact with the officer, so I played along and did the same. "Uptown," Julius said. "We're headed back that way."

"Maybe you oughta stay up there, too," said the officer. "I heard that one of you rats was causin' a commotion down by the hotel. We don't need the likes of you hooligans in this neighborhood. And wherever you found this gypsy," he snorted, waving his nightstick in my direction, "you oughta send him right back."

"Yes, sir," Adolph whispered, still looking straight ahead.

Just then the man behind the counter handed us three glasses with a fizzy, foamy red drink in them.

"I'll get it," I said, and reached into my pocket and pulled out the twenty that my Mom had given me…that morning and 104 years in the future. "Can you break a twenty?"

The soda jerk's eyes got wide. "Twenny simoleons!" he gasped. "Jumpin' Jehosaphat! Will you take a look at dot! Is dot even real?"

The air in the room seemed to suddenly go totally dry and silent. I realized too late that I had just made another terrible mistake, and I should have handed over Omar's quarter instead. "Put that away," Julius hissed at me. "That's more money than this copper makes in a month."

A heavy hand landed on my shoulder. It hurt, and I squirmed under it. It was the police officer and he was holding me roughly. "Now where's a little street rat like you gettin' to have a note like that?" he asked. "And wouldn't I like to know why you aren't in school? Or maybe you should be warkin' upstate in the mills, shouldn't ya? Now hand it over, ya thieving little gypsy."

"My mom gave me the money," I stammered. "And I'm just visiting here. I'm…I'm…"

"FROM OREGON!" the two Marx brothers shouted in unison.

And then everything started to happen very fast. Adolph slid under the policeman's arm and wedged himself between me and the cop, breaking the cop's grip on my shoulder. The policeman snatched the twenty-dollar bill from me, but Julius reached over and snatched it right back out of his hand. Then he grabbed me and pulled me backwards, away from the cop and his brother.

"Josh!" he hissed in my ear as he stuffed the twenty back into my hoodie pocket. "Run!"

"What?"

"RUN! BEAT IT! SCRAM!"

He pushed me in the direction of the door just as Adolph grabbed the policeman's big blue hat with both hands and yanked it down over his eyes. The policeman swung wildly with the nightstick, but Adolph ducked it and crawled on all fours towards the door. The cop swung again and this time the nightstick whizzed over Adolph's head and smashed into one of the glass jars of juice, sending it flying in a million pieces as the juice gushed onto the counter and floor, which caused the cop to slip and fall. That's all I saw before Julius pushed me out the door.

Then the three of us were on the street and booking it as fast as we could, up Fifth Avenue. We could hear the loud shriek of the policeman's whistle behind us, but the sound faded the further north we got. We didn't stop for breath until we had crossed Forty-Second Street.

"What . . . was that . . . all about?" I gasped, trying to catch my breath.

"Kid, I don't care what planet you're from, you never wave that kind of money around," Julius said.

"Especially not to a bull," Adolph added.

"A bull?"

"A copper like that who is on the take," Julius explained. "See, they find runaway kids like you, deliver them to the factory agents for a finder's fee, and the next thing you know you're being packed upstate to work in the textile mills, and nobody ever sees you again. And your twenty-dollar note lands right in that copper's back pocket."

"They can do that?" I gasped. "Isn't child labor illegal?"

The two of them just stared at me like I was from Mars. A streetcar was boarding near us, and Julius and Adolph stuffed me onto it and then jumped on. "Sure, it's illegal," Julius said, shooting a knowing look at Adolph as the streetcar began to rattle its way north.

And then they both said in unison, "If you're FROM OREGON."

I slumped down in my seat, wondering what to do. "Now it's time to come clean," Julius said to me, "and if I had a bar of soap handy, I'd clean you myself."

Adolph nodded and said, "It's okay, Josh. You can tell us where you're really from. What happened? Are you an orphan?" He looked so sincere and he was just so nice that I instinctively trusted him.

"It's kind of a long story," I said. "And I'm not a runaway, or an orphan. Well, not exactly. Technically, my parents won't be born for another seventy-five years."

Julius whistled and reached into his pocket, pulled out another cigar, and this time lit it. None of the other people on the streetcar said a word of complaint about the smelly cigar. Most of the men on board were smoking.

"It's okay, Josh," he said, "it's a long way to Ninety-Third Street. And if you need more time, we'll just make a couple of loops around Manhattan Island." He sat back and crossed his ankles in front of him and raised his eyebrows while faking a big, dreamy smile. "Why, we have all the time in the world. The night is young and life is grand! The sun is shining and Mammy is making a shoo-fly pie and we don't have a care. Tra la la!"

Then his eyes narrowed and he fixed his gaze on me. "Begin," said Julius Marx. "And don't forget to start with Once Upon a Time."

Adolph Marx sat next to him, patiently waiting for me to start talking. He reached into his pocket, and if there had been any doubt before that I was sitting before the great Harpo Marx, albeit a much younger version of Harpo than ever appeared in the movies I saw, the next thing he did erased it completely.

He reached into his pocket and squeezed something. HONK! went the taxi horn that he had been hiding inside his coat. He rolled his eyes and did it again. HONK HONK! The people near us on the streetcar looked around for the source of the sound and he pretended that he didn't know a thing about it. When they looked away he did it again. HONK! The lady sitting next to him jumped three inches. He looked at her, gave her a big, leering grin and wiggled his eyebrows, and she got to her feet and walked away to the other end of the car.

I smiled. Despite being scared, lost, nervous and a little hungry, I was also more than a little bit thrilled. Because I was sitting next to and had the rapt attention of two of the funniest men in history. And we were going to their house.

"Okay," I said, "Here goes. Once upon a time, and about six hours ago, I played a little joke on my substitute language arts teacher."

Julius grinned. "Ah, a joker," he said. "Why, I like this story already. Adolph, I think we have a winner here."

Adolph Marx didn't say anything. But his hand moved in his pocket, and he HONK HONKED out a yes.

Julius grinned and raised his eyebrows. "What's with the trombone?" he asked his brother.

"Just found this horn tossed onto the side of the road this morning," said Adolph. "I have no idea what to do with it, but it's pretty fun, isn't it?"

Julius nodded. "Yes it is. Indeed it is. Why, you could annoy half the borough of Manhattan with that thing before the sun sets."

Adolph grinned, too, and honked again twice, which he had just decided meant yes.

I smiled, too, but I was suddenly overcome with a feeling of dread. Where, exactly, was I? Even better, *when* was I? And how would I ever get back to my own time? Old Slivers was a little short on details other than I just had a few days to accomplish my task. And finally, as we crossed East 65th Street and the trolley continued to rattle uptown, what in the world was a Comedy Keeper, and who had appointed me, young Josh Markowitz, to become one?

I looked at Julius and then at Adolph. "Okay, for starters," I said, "do you guys realize how funny you actually are?"

HONK HONK was the immediate answer.

CHAPTER TEN: FROM THE DIARY OF OMAR SPARROW

The first thing I did when I found out that Josh was missing and had stood up Elizabeth Walcot Woolcott was to ride my bike over to his house. His mom answered the door and I lied like a living-room carpet and told Mrs. Markowitz that Josh had gone off camping with the Patton Middle School Boy Scout troupe. "Camping?" she said. "I didn't even know that Josh liked camping."

"I know, right?" I said. "I think he's only in it for the s'mores."

She shook her head. "Kids," she said.

I shook mine and agreed. "Kids."

I told her lie number two, that they'd be back in a few days, before spring break was over, and not to bother to call or text Josh, because Boy Scouts (lie number three, but who's counting?) camp off the grid. That's how they roll, I said with a straight face.

Then I got back on my bike and convened a meeting at the Patton tennis courts that consisted of me, Jackson, Elizabeth W.W., and stupid Stevie SanPedro, who insisted on horning in even though he wasn't invited. I invited Amy C., too, but Elizabeth said that she was busy – "watching telly," whatever that means -- and couldn't make it but she would tell her everything we said.

"Maybe Fartowitz got abducted by aliens," sneered Stevie.

Elizabeth shot him a withering look and said, "Oh DO shut up, Steven." And for once, he did.

I told them everything I knew. That Josh told me he was going downtown to see some clown who could get him out of detention. A quick poll of the group revealed that nobody had ever heard of a clown or a magic shop in McMinnville. I felt terrible. What kind of best friend lets his buddy ride off alone into a bad neighborhood to meet with a mysterious clown?

"I should have gone with him," I said.

Stevie snorted. "You think?"

"Don't blame yourself," said Elizabeth. "I'm quite sure that Jawsh will be just fine."

"Is there anything else he said or did that was unusual?" asked Jackson.

"Yeah," I said, "he was holding a pair of those fake nose and eyeglasses, with the built-in moustache and eyebrows. Said the clown had left them behind."

"They're called Groucho glasses," said Elizabeth. "Quite posh in the UK at one time. I can't imagine why."

We agreed to stick together, got on our bikes and rode downtown. We rode past six creepy old warehouses, up two just-as-creepy alleys and down a gravel side street. And then we spotted it. Josh's bike was leaned against a building that looked like it hadn't seen the hand of humans for about 200 years. The windows were either smashed in or boarded up, there were weeds taller than me covering the front door and the paint was either peeling away or gone altogether. It was as spooky a place as I've ever seen, and that counts the Haunted House on Third Street every Halloween.

"I'm not going in there," cried out Stevie. He turned about fifty shades of white and then, without another word, he turned his bike around and high-tailed it out of there. We last saw him hunched over the handlebars and peddling furiously back over the railroad tracks. Chicken! Throw some feed to the chicken! Cluck cluck cluck!!

The doors were all locked and the place was dark inside, so we found a window in the back that we could open, and climbed in. So besides becoming a liar all of a sudden, I've also begun to experiment with burglary, and breaking and entering. What a spring break I'm having, diary!

The place looked like it hadn't seen the light of day for, like, a hundred years. It was dark and cluttered with junk, and dusty. There was no sign of the clown who owned the place, and no answer when we asked if anyone was there. We looked around, and then suddenly Elizabeth gasped. "Are these the ones, Omar?" she asked. (When she says my name, she pronounces it, "Omah.") She was holding the Groucho glasses up.

I nodded. "Yeah, those are the ones." I felt terrible. What had happened to Josh?

Just then a loud, buzzing sound went off near us and we all nearly jumped out of our skins, and then clung to each other like frightened kittens in a tight little hug. Jackson was the first to disengage, and he went to the sound. He came back holding Josh's cell phone, which was *still buzzing. The caller ID said it was his mom calling.*

"Don't answer it," I hissed. "I told her Josh was out camping."

"Good show, Omah," said Elizabeth. "Why tell his parents the truth when Josh is missing and might have been kidnapped from this bloody, awful place? Gone camping. That's rather classic." She started to sniffle, wiped her nose with her sleeve and said to herself, "Stiff upper lip. Mustn't weep. Iron Maiden and all that rot."

I looked past her and that's when I saw that the weird old magician's box thing seemed to have some of the dust wiped away from it. The Great Wandini, it said in faded letters on the side of the box. I ran my fingers up and down the case that held the magician's turbaned head, trying to find clues, and when I put my hand on the weird stick in front of it, the whole thing lit up.

"Freakin' awesome," gasped Jackson.

"What do I do?" I groaned. To tell you the truth, diary, I was scared half out of my mind.

"You ask it a question," said Elizabeth. "See, it says on the side that he'll answer any question."

I gripped the handle tighter. "Great Wandini," I said, "where's Josh?"

The magician's head inside the box swiveled from side to side, his stupid grin not budging, and then a slip of paper popped out of the side of the machine and fell to the floor by our feet. Elizabeth grabbed it.

"It says, 'Ask another time.'

Ask who? Ask when? I tried desperately to remember the name of the guy who Josh said he was going to see. Spanky? Sunshine? Stirrups? "I can't remember the clown's name," I groaned.

"So ask the magician," said Jackson. "Duh. It says to ask him anything."

"Great Wandini," I said, still holding the hand on the end of the stick, "what was the name of the clown who was here before?"

The head turned from side to side again, and the paper that popped out said, "Be careful you don't get Slivers."

That was it! Slivers the Clown!

I was mulling this over when Elizabeth suddenly shoved me aside, and grabbed the handle of the Great Wandini herself. "Now listen here," she said in a commanding voice, "enough of this…polly-woggling. You tell us at once where we can find this Slivers the Clown. And Jawsh, too."

The head swiveled and the paper that popped out only said, "You call yourself posh?"

She gripped the handle harder and shouted, "I said at once!"

This time the head moved slowly from side to side, and we could hear gears creaking and wood groaning. It barely had enough power to pop out one more scrap of paper, and then The Great Wandini went dark.

"Horsefeathers and Nightingales," was all the paper said.

We looked at each other. "What's that supposed to mean?" asked Jackson.

"I'm bolloxed if I know," said Elizabeth.

"What she said," I added.

Elizabeth began to sniffle again, and tears began to run down her cheeks. Jackson patted her on the back, and so did I. She shook her head and wiped her face with her sleeve.

"Josh could be anywhere," she whispered. "He's totally gone missing."

Jackson looked at me with his eyebrows raised. He silently mouthed words so she wouldn't hear him. "What the heck did she just say?"

I also felt like crying. Don't know why I didn't. "It means that Josh is gone," I said. "He's just like totally gone. And we have no idea how to find him or where to look."

We agreed that it was getting dark and awfully creepy in that warehouse and we all had to get home, and would meet up the next day to figure out what to do after we had some time to think about it.

Horsefeathers and Nightingales. What in the world could that mean?

Short answer: In McMinnville in 2012, not a whole lot.

Best thing to come of all this, diary? When I called Elizabeth later that night to see if she was okay, Amy Connors answered the phone. "Lizzie's taking a long bubble bath right now, and acting out all of the parts in Mary Poppins," she said. "But why don't you meet me at Serendipity tomorrow and tell me everything? I'll buy you an ice-cream."

Josh was sweet on E.W.W., but I always liked her cousin Amy better. This was going to work out great.

I mean, if we can ever get Josh back, maybe we'll double-date then.

CHAPTER ELEVEN: COMING CLEAN, SORT OF

But where to start? "Okay, look," I said, "you may not believe a word of this, but just hear me out." Julius and Adolph exchanged a glance, and then nodded for me to continue as the streetcar lurched and rattled up the street.

I cleared my throat and started by telling them that I had indeed come from Oregon, but it was the Oregon of 2012 – I was from the future. I told them that *Duck Soup*, which they wouldn't even make for another twenty-five years, was one of my grandfather's favorite movies ever, and that besides the two of them, it featured their brothers Chico and Zeppo. I pronounced the first one Chick-o, not Cheek-o, as I had learned from my grandfather.

"Two more Marx Brothers of whom I've never heard," grumbled Julius.

"Maybe he means Leonard. I can see someone calling him Chick-o," said Adolph. "All he ever does is chase chicks."

"And other assorted birdies," added Julius. "Leonard's our big brother, Josh. He's a womanizer and a gambler and about the last person I'd ever picture being in the movies. Why, the thought of it tickles me silly." He did a fake little giggle. "And by Zeppo, maybe you mean one of my little brothers, Milton or Herbert. But they're just kids. Herb's seven years old. You're telling me that he's a movie idol, too?"

"He won't be seven years old forever," I reminded him. "And he won't become as big of a star as you three. You, Adolph and Leonard – who are called Groucho, Harpo and Chico – are the real draw. You will make some of the funniest, zaniest movies ever. Dazzling wordplay, big musical numbers, crazy situations. That leaves one more brother, who also appears in your shows. His name is Gummo."

Adolph laughed. "He must be talking about Milton. He's always creeping around like a gumshoe detective."

Julius raised his eyebrows and shot Adolph a look. "Well, if you're so smart, what about our sister? Doesn't she make it onto the big screen, too?"

I shook my head. "Sorry, Julius, but you don't have a sister. Nice try."

For once he didn't say a word. He took a couple of puffs from the cigar and then shook his head in disbelief. "Well, that settles that, doesn't it? The Marx Brothers get the dopiest names in show business –

Grouchy, Harpy, Gummy. And kid, did you say something about music? Are you telling me that the movies where you come from have sound?"

The brothers looked at each other and said in unison, "IN OREGON?" And Harpo honked his horn.

I had to laugh, they were just so naturally funny and in synch with each other. "Yup," I said, nodding my head. "I can't remember when they figured out...I mean, will figure out...how to synch sound and dialogue and the picture, but they will soon. Have you ever heard of Al Jolson?"

"Of course. The vaudeville star," said Julius. "He makes a fortune on the circuit."

"Well, he will make the first talking movie, called *The Jazz Singer*. Don't ask me when. I never was very good at history class."

"Well you've got me beat," said Groucho. "I was never very good with class, period. I left school when I was thirteen years old. And I've always regretted it." He sighed and puffed on his cigar.

I pressed on. "And color, too. The movies will get something called Technicolor. But that won't happen for, like, another fifty years. Oh, and Harpo...I mean Adolph...never talks in the movies. He does everything through mime and funny sound effects. When he's not playing his harp, I mean."

At that, Adolph let out a long whistle, another HONK from his horn, and then sat back in his seat, stunned.

Julius grinned and chomped on his cigar. "Somebody better tell Mary Pickford and Douglas Fairbanks that they can open their mouths and start yakkin'." He laughed and blew a smoke ring at the roof of the streetcar.

"The Marx Brothers as talking movie stars. Why, that's the craziest thing I've ever heard."

The brothers asked me questions about the future all the way uptown as the streetcar rattled along Lexington Avenue. But I could tell that they didn't really believe me, they were just humoring me in the way that adults do with kids. And I couldn't blame them: Trying to explain television, computers, the internet and Netflix to people who had never even heard a radio was like if someone showed up on your doorstep and started to babble about flying babies and interstellar teleportation. You'd think they were a few fries short of a Happy Meal, too.

I tried to keep it as simple as possible, but like any struggling comedian, I could tell that I was losing my audience. I made about as much sense to them as a four-year old kid declaring that he's Spiderman.

We were nearing Eighty-Fifth Street and an area where the houses were all dilapidated tenements, wedged next to each other side by side, with garbage all over the sidewalks, when Groucho turned to me with a serious expression on his face.

"Well, Josh from Oregon, this is all very interesting, and you sure have one wild and vivid imagination," he said. "But why are you telling us this? What's in it for you? What's your racket, kid?"

I blushed. I had gotten so caught up in the experience of being with the young Marx Brothers that I had forgotten why I was there. "I was sent here to help you," I said. "To help you become comedians. I heard that you're stuck, and not sure what to do. You're on the verge of something. I don't know how or why, but at this very moment your lives could go one way or the other. Julius, you can either be loved by millions and called one of the great comics of the 20th century. Or you can become a tailor like your dad and keep your friends amused with your fine jokes. Adolph, that brilliant comedy that you just showed downtown at the hotel can go on to entertain the whole world. Or you can just live your life as a nice guy who has a hard time keeping a job. Believe me, I don't understand this either, it's just what I was told. Seemed to make sense at the time…"

My voice trailed off. I was starting to not believe it myself. What Slivers had told me suddenly seemed crazy and out of this world. For that matter, so was Slivers, now that I stopped to think about it.

"And there's one more thing," I said. "I only have a week to make you become comedians. So how about it. Why don't you start being funny on stage right now?"

Julius whistled and Adolph pursed his lips and nodded. They both stood up because we were nearing our stop. Julius looked at me sadly. "Just like that, huh? We throw away our careers as singers because Josh from Oregon shows up and tells us we should be comics.

"Wish I could help you, Josh," he continued, "but I'm afraid you've come to the wrong place. You see, we're not comedians at all. You got it right that we're performers, but we're singers. Why, I've been on the road since I was your age, singing on stage, and that's what I intend to keep doing until I'm old and toothless and they call me Old Pappy." He made a face with his lips wrapped around his teeth to look like an old man.

Adolph nodded. "Singers and musicians. Our mother makes us practice our music every day. We play the vaudeville circuit. I don't know how you knew that I play the harp. I just started a few months ago. Lucky guess, maybe. And my brother Leonard is a piano player who has never told a joke in his life."

Julius hopped off the streetcar and looked up at me. "That's right. We couldn't tell a joke on stage to save our lives. Never have and never will. Hey Josh, do me a favor?"

I felt crushed, like someone had punched me in the stomach and knocked out all of my wind. My heart sank and my feet suddenly felt like lead. Had I come all this way for nothing?

"Sure," I mumbled. "Name it."

"If you find some other Marx Brothers who do comedy, let us know, will ya? I'd like to see their act. Thanks for the story, Josh. It was certainly interesting."

Adolph honked his horn in agreement.

They were walking away, and I was still on the streetcar. I felt it lurch into motion and I suddenly felt utterly lost. I didn't know where I was, and for the first time since I arrived that morning, I didn't even know WHEN I was. And it hit me like a ton of bricks that I didn't have a clue how to get back to my own time. Slivers had failed to mention that little detail. "Text me," he had said, as if that were somehow possible in 1908. I reached into my pocket and felt the token that he had slipped me just as I was about to travel back through time. Cool. I had a token. But I had no idea what to do with it.

But reaching into my pocket gave me a sudden idea. I jumped off the streetcar and almost fell flat on my face from the momentum, but caught myself just in time. I reached into my pocket.

"Guys!" I called after Julius and Adolph. "Guys? Hey, Marx Brothers!"

They stopped and I ran up to them. "If I was lying, and made that all up," I said, "how would I have gotten this?"

I pulled out the quarter that Omar had given me and showed it to them. Good old George Washington in a wig on the front, and on the back, the year 2012 stamped into the metal.

Julius shook his head. "Why I'll be a monkey's uncle," he said softly. "Where in blazes did you get that, Josh?"

"From my friend, Omar. This morning. In 2012."

They exchanged another knowing look, and Adolph put his arm around me. "Whether you're lying or telling the truth, you still need a hot meal. Come on, Josh, you're coming home with us."

Julius nodded. "I don't care if you're from Oregon, the future, or if you're a Katzenjammer Kid," he said. "You wouldn't last ten minutes in this neighborhood dressed like that. Lucky for you, I know a good tailor. Well actually, he's a lousy tailor. But I dare you to do better."

We walked a few blocks. There were no cars in this part of town, just more horses and buggies. The buildings looked older, and some sagged dangerously. Julius suddenly stopped dead in his tracks. Adolph looked up and then hissed at me, in a low voice, "Josh, freeze." He grabbed me by the sleeve of my hoodie and pulled me off the sidewalk and under the awning of a store. "It's him," he whispered again. "He followed us."

I peeked out from where he was hiding, and saw what he was talking about. That same police officer who had chased us downtown was standing just a few feet away, so close that I could read his name tag: Mulcahy. He was peering around, obviously trying to find someone.

Adolph let out a low whistle, and down the street, where he had also frozen and tried to melt into the landscape, Julius responded with four low whistles. Adolph's grip on my sleeve tightened. "This isn't good," he whispered in my ear. "There are four of them." He jerked his head to the side and nodded to where three men were standing, also looking around like they were trying to find someone. They wore shabby suits and ties and top hats, not police uniforms like Mulcahy.

"Who are they?" I breathed, as quietly as I could, into Adolph's ear. "What do they want?"

"Factory agents," he whispered back. "They look for kids to sell upriver to work in the mills."

There was another whistle from Julius, and Adolph nodded and whistled back. "Remember this address," he whispered to me. "One seventy-nine East Ninety-Third Street. Apartment 4F. When I tell you, you run as fast as your legs can carry you and wait for us there. Got it?"

I nodded. "Got it."

"Josh," he said, his eyes wide and bulging, "this is no joke. If they catch you, you're done for, and we won't be able to help you."

Then I saw Julius cross the street, walking directly towards the factory agents. "Say, fellas," he said in a loud stage voice, "I wonder if you can help me. Why, I think I've lost a button on my coat and maybe you know someone in the clothing business who can fix it."

At the sound of his voice, Officer Mulcahy jumped nearly a foot and raised his whistle to his mouth. He was about to blow it, alerting any other police in the area that there was a disturbance, but just then Adolph jumped in front of him and began honking his horn. When Mulcahy turned to face him, Adolph grabbed the whistle right out of his mouth. "Run!" he yelled to me, and then took off in the opposite direction as the big cop gave chase.

I ran as fast as I could, reading the numbers on the street signs, and then the building numbers on East Ninety-Third Street, on the fly. I didn't stop until I found the building marked 179. I entered the foyer, found the staircase, and ran all the way up to 4F. I knocked on the door and waited. Nothing happened. So I pounded hard on it.

A funny looking little man with a thin moustache and slicked-back hair opened the door a crack, peered out at me, and said in a thick German accent, "Vell? Vaht's da trouble?"

I had to catch my breath. "Groucho and Harpo...I mean Julius and Adolph...sent me," I said between gasps of air.

"Chulius und Adolph zent you?"

"Yes!"

The little man sighed. "Minnie," he called out over his shoulder, "varm up ze coffee. Ve've got another rascal."

He opened the door wider and motioned me to come in. As I passed him, he peered nervously past me down the hall, and then closed and locked the door behind us.

CHAPTER TWELVE: GROUCH BAG

Being at home with the Marx family, I quickly learned, was very much like being an extra in the middle of a Marx Brothers movie. You stand there holding your shield or pretending to be a cabin steward on a cruise ship and try to not laugh your head off every single minute as the brothers careen around the room, bouncing off of every surface, insulting anyone and everyone and generally having a blast.

Frenchie and Minnie were the brothers' parents. Frenchie was a little man with thin, gray hair slicked straight back on his head who wore a suit and tie, even at home, and sat in the corner of their three-room apartment in a big chair, reading the newspaper and trying to ignore the mayhem swirling around him. His real name was Sam and he spoke with a thick accent that I later learned was from where he grew up in the German-speaking part of eastern France, hence his nickname. He was a tailor by trade and as I stood there, he gaped at me and my modern clothes up and down.

He had never seen anything like a hoodie and a pair of Nikes before. Julius and Adolph arrived moments later, out of breath. They had completely outrun the cop and factory agents before dashing home.

Frenchie reached out and rubbed his fingers on the sleeve of my cotton/poly hoodie and muttered, "Dot's nice material." Then he pulled out a measuring tape and began to measure my arms, legs and waist. He rummaged through a heap of clothes on the floor in the corner of the room and came out with a whole suit for me: Pants, long suit jacket, a tie, a woolen cap and a white shirt that was kind of faded and bluish-gray, made in a rough, scratchy material.

"See, I told you he was a lousy tailor," said Julius when I tried on the clothes and found that one pants leg, and the opposite arm of the shirt, were short by a good two inches. "But at least now you don't look like you stepped straight off the circus train."

Minnie Marx, their mother, was a short, round woman with brown hair pulled back in a bun and sharp, brown eyes that didn't seem to miss anything. She sized me up immediately and said to Julius, "This one's trouble. Why do you always have to bring trouble into our home? We don't have enough trouble, already?" But she was just kidding him, and her eyes were kind and welcoming to me as she said it. She put her hand on my elbow and steered me to a chair in the corner. "Sit," she said. "You need something to eat."

Julius jumped to his feet, walked up behind her, put his arms around her and started dancing with her from behind. "It's because I love you, don't you understand?" he crooned to her like they were in a movie doing a love scene. "Say it. Oh, Minnie. Minnie. Say that you love me too and we'll fly straight to the moon. Or straight to Canarsie. I couldn't afford the moon, but who could at these prices?"

"Ack!" she yelled, pulling his hands off her. "I'll send you to the moon all right, with a swift kick!" She was laughing. Sam went into the kitchen and five minutes later brought me a bowl of steaming chicken soup that was the best I've ever eaten. I didn't realize it, but I was starving, and when I finished the bowl, he brought me another.

As I sat and ate the soup, the two younger brothers, Milton and Herbert came in. They immediately started up a mock battle of sword-fighting with Julius, who leaped on the couch, jumped around and yelled things like, "Avast ye scurvy dogs! I strike at thee!"

"Right boys," said Minnie, clapping her hands, "it's time to practice your music. We have a show on Sunday, so let's get to it."

Julius explained to me, as he warmed up his voice with a series of vocal exercises, that the family had a singing act that played in a vaudeville theater out in Coney Island. The act was called the Four

Nightingales, and consisted of Julius, Milton, Adolph and a family friend named Lou Levy. "That's where the real money is, Josh," he confided. "I mean, I thought once about doing comedy, like you suggested, but Mom's against it. 'You're only funny to some people, mostly yourselves,' she always says. 'But everybody loves a good song.'

"And Josh," he continued, "I've been singing for a living since I was your age. All over the country, moving from one fleabag hotel to another to make a buck. I kind of wished I could have stayed in school and learned a thing or two, but performing was where the money was, and the family needed it. And when Minnie started the Four Nightingales and got us some bookings, well, that kind of settled it once and for all."

"But look at you guys!" I nearly shouted at him. "You're the funniest thing I've ever seen. You should be doing comedy on-stage, not singing."

He shrugged. "It's Minnie's act, and she calls the shots. Besides, we're only funny around each other. I'm not so sure that the world is ready for the Marx Brothers. Uh oh, speaking of funny business, Josh, watch your wallet. Here comes trouble."

Another person came into the room, shorter than the others, and a few years older, but unmistakably a Marx brother. "Josh," said Julius, "meet Leonard. Lenny, meet the pride of Oregon." He then circled the side of his head with his finger, cocked his head in my direction, and said in a stage whisper, "He's from the future!"

"Hey, nice to meet you Josh," said Leonard. The voice, the eyes…I had seen him perform in movies, and always knew him as Chico, or Chick-o, the wiliest of the Marx Brothers. He generally played a con man character with a thick Italian accent, and his comedy was always about rapid-fire wordplay, outrageous puns and crazy situations. When the plots of the movies bogged down, he was always good for a scene where he played the piano in a breezy, funny way or talked a straight man out of his money.

"So you're from the future, huh?" he said, and I decided on the spot to play along.

"No, I'm past that," I said quickly. "I left the future behind me, right around Seventy-Seventh Street."

"That's-a too bad," he said, slipping right into the Italian accent that I knew from his movies. "If you'd-a waited to 80th Street you could'a got an advance on the future. You go straight to 1923 and get a nickel. And if you wait until 85th you get another nickel and a new pair-a pants. Now you gotta two nickels, but you gotta go back to 1823. Right, boss?"

He turned to Julius, who said, "Don't look at me. It doesn't make a lick of century."

"Hey, dot's a good one," said Leonard, pulling a tissue from his sleeve and handing it to Julius. "Here's-a you tissue. It works better if you get down on your sneeze. And that's a nice crease in them trousers, you must be a member of the press."

The brothers all laughed. Leonard clapped me on the back. "You're gonna fit in just fine around here, Josh," he said in his normal voice.

In the corner of the room, Frenchie had been quietly looking over my clothes from the 21st century, caressing the material and closely examining the stitching, and he suddenly shouted out, "Holy cats! Will you have a look at dis!"

He pulled out the twenty-dollar bill that had been in my pocket and waved it around. "I've never held one of dese in my own fingers!"

Leonard strode over, took the bill from his father's hand, examined both sides of it and then gave me a long, careful look, as if he were seeing me for the first time. "Julie," he said, "you'd better get him a grouch bag."

"Lennie, no."

"You heard me. He needs to protect his money better. Go get it."

Julius disappeared into the back room and came back a moment later with what looked like a little, cloth purse with a zipper and a long string attached to two corners of it. He handed it reluctantly over to Leonard.

"Josh, do you know what this is?" asked the eldest brother. "This is called a grouch bag. All of the performers on the road have one. You use it to keep your valuables safe and close to you at all times. You never let them out of your sight or off of your person. Let me show you how it works."

From the couch, Julius said, "It's called a grouch bag because it makes you grouchy, having that thing rubbing against your skin all day long. Believe me, I know the feeling. I've been wearing one of those things on the road since I was nine years old."

Leonard carefully took my twenty-dollar bill, folded it in half, unzipped the pocket of the grouch bag and put it inside, then zipped the pocket back up. He did this very deliberately and made sure I was watching every movement. Then he slipped the cord over his neck and stuck the bag inside his shirt.

"See?" he said. "That's how it works. You never let your grouch bag leave your sight. Keep it close to your chest and you won't lose your money." He reached inside his shirt, pulled the bag out and handed it to me.

I thanked him and put the bag around my neck and stuffed it under my shirt so nobody could see it. Leonard turned and started walking towards the door, as if he was in a sudden hurry to leave. But then, across the room, Minnie's voice rang out. The Marx Brothers' mom was unmistakably angry.

"Leonard!"

"Aw, Mom," he said, like a little boy who was caught with his hand in the cookie jar.

"You give that back!"

"I was just trying to teach the kid a thing or two," he whined. She glared at him, her finger pointed accusingly at her eldest son. He sighed and came back into the room.

"Okay, Josh, look inside your grouch bag," he said to me.

I reached into my shirt, pulled out the bag and looked inside. It was stuffed with tissue paper. I looked harder. The twenty-dollar bill was nowhere in sight. "How in the world did you do that?" I asked.

"That's the oldest trick in the book that you just fell for," said Adolph, who had left his harp and come into the room. "Josh, you've just been a victim of the pigeon drop."

"The kid needed to learn something," said Leonard, again with a defensive whine in his voice. "And now he has."

"See," said Adolph, "Lennie had another grouch bag exactly the same as yours hidden under his shirt. And when he put your grouch bag inside his shirt, he just pulled the other bag out, and it was full of nothing. You were the pigeon, and that was the drop. You never for a second knew that your money was under his shirt, not yours. If this had happened on the street, he'd be long gone by the time you figured it out."

"Here's your twenty bucks," said Leonard, handing me the real bag with my bill in it. "Don't be a sucker," he grinned, patting me on the cheek. His grin was so genuine and infectious that I just couldn't be mad at him.

"See, Minnie," he said, crossing the room to give her a big hug and kiss, "I was just teaching the kid an important lesson."

"You little *pisher*," she said, giving him a push on the chest. "Someday someone's going to teach you an important lesson."

"I'll never learn," he grinned, and kissed her again. "I can't stay. Big card game brewing uptown tonight." He stopped to look me up and down carefully. "From the future, huh? We should talk. I bet we could make lotsa money together."

He went into the tiny kitchen, grabbed a hunk of dark bread and a piece of cheese, stuffed it into his mouth and was gone as quickly as he had arrived.

All night long, as I lie awake on a mattress on the floor surrounded by the other boys, I found myself patting my grouch bag, or taking it out to check if my money was still in it. I added Omar's quarter to the bag for safe-keeping, zipped it up and stuffed it back under my shirt. I pulled the rough blanket over me, rearranged the pillow that was a handful of leftover fabric scraps, and tried to sleep. It was my first night sleeping in the past, and I missed my mom and dad and warm, comfortable bed. Was this what I got for being the Class Clown? I'd settle for just getting my picture in the yearbook. At that moment I seriously wondered if being funny was worth the trouble it could cause a guy. I had never understood it when my uncle warned me that there was a dark side to having a great sense of humor, a sadness behind it. But maybe I was getting little glimpses of that now.

I must have dozed off because when I opened my eyes again it was very dark and still in the room, the two younger brothers were sleeping soundly beside me, and I could hear muffled voices coming from the room next door. If I put my ear to the wall I could hear what they were saying.

"He's obviously lying. What's his racket?" It was Minnie's muffled voice coming from the kitchen, where Minnie, Sam and the three older brothers were meeting.

"How can we be so sure? Edgar Cayce says that crazy stuff like this happens all the time." It was Julius voice. "Just because we don't believe in time travel doesn't mean it's not possible. I don't believe in Teddy Roosevelt, for example, but he keeps insisting that he's the President."

"Yeah," chimed in Leonard, "you know, Julius has a point, even if it's on the top of his head."

"Let's not be foolish," said Minnie. "People don't just pop up out of nowhere with a fake quarter and a phony piece of paper. I've held a twenty-dollar note before, and it doesn't look like that."

There was a pause and then Adolph said softly, "You have?"

"Well I'd like to hold one or two of them one day myself," said Julius, "and I'm not so sure that's going to happen if we keep singing on vaudeville for peanuts."

"Yeah, Ma," said Leonard. "Why not give comedy a try? What do we have to lose?"

Minnie snorted. "What do we have to lose? I'll tell you what we have to lose. If you're not funny the first minute you walk out there we lose the whole career that we've worked so hard on for these last ten years. Everything. Down the drain. Are you going to risk this whole family's future on a...on a whim from some kid who drops down from the sky?"

Adolph spoke up. "Comedy is hard. We've all seen how Uncle Al has had his ups and downs. It changes all the time what people think is funny. And I sure don't see myself telling jokes and waiting for laughs. I'd be scared to death on that stage."

"Exactly," said Minnie, slapping the table for emphasis. "Everybody loves a good song. A joke goes away with the breeze. You have no idea how hard it is to sustain a career in comedy."

And then Leonard's voice said, almost mournfully, "But we're funny, Ma. I know that deep down in my heart."

Julius piped in, "Yes we are. Sometimes I'm in stitches while I'm wearing Frenchie's stitches."

"You see," said Minnie, "that's what I mean. Nobody would get your jokes. Our funny stuff is best shared inside this apartment. The outside world wouldn't get them. And there would be nothing that would break this mother's heart more than to see my boys lay a big, fat egg up on that stage and get booed all the way back to Poughkeepsie."

Another pause. "That's a long way to be booed, Poughkeepsie," said Leonard.

"I'd rather have rotten eggs thrown at me in Queens than be booed in Poughkeepsie," said Julius, pretending to shiver with fear.

"Zo, how do vee handle zis mischief?" asked Sam.

"Leave it to me," said Leonard. "I've been around con artists before. I know how to handle them. I'll get to the truth about this kid Josh. Let me ask around about him on the streets. Somebody must have seen him before."

There were a few audible sighs. And then Julius said softly, "Well, just don't hurt the kid. I kind of like him."

"Me too," said Adolph.

"What, hurt the kid?" said Leonard. "I wouldn't touch a hair on his head."

"It's not his head I'm worried about," snapped Julius. "I'm more concerned with you getting into his pockets. Or selling him to the gypsies to settle a bet that you lost."

Minnie cleared her throat. "That's a fine sentiment, my wonderful boys. But number one rule is don't hurt the family. We stick together, right? The Marx family has always done it together. Right?"

"I guess."

"Right, Mama."

"Sure."

"Ja, of course."

"Now let's get some sleep," she said. "We have a show coming up. A singing show. And my little nightingales have to be at the top of their voice. I wore through the soles of my shoes looking up agents who could get us this booking. Don't spoil it for your Mama. If we do well on Sunday the Four Nightingales can count on steady bookings through the summer."

I rolled over and pretended to sleep. They thought I was a big fake who was trying to con them? I've never been more scared in my life. "Slivers," I whispered into my pillow, "I need you."

Why did I have to be so funny? Mr. Yanuzzi's basement was nothing compared to this. Why me?

CHAPTER THIRTEEN: FROM THE DIARY OF OMAR SPARROW

I spent a night tossing and turning in bed, wondering what to do to find Josh. Where could he be? Nothing came to me until about twenty minutes before the morning alarm rang, but it came to me good and strong. I did my morning chores, kissed my mom goodbye and then at the stroke of ten, I took the scraps of paper from The Great Wandini straight to the library, got on a computer terminal and began to punch in things. It took a few hours of figuring things out on the computer and going down a few blind alleys, as it always does, but I finally got it.

First I Googled the words horsefeathers and Groucho glasses, and I learned all that I ever need to know about a comedy family called the Marx Brothers. They made a bunch of movies and were popular about a million years ago. I watched a couple of clips of them on YouTube and they were funny in a goofy, black-and-white way.

I tried to look up Slivers, and spent a half-hour wading through articles about digging bits of wood out of your skin with needles. But then I changed the search to Slivers, Clown, and bingo. I found out that Frank "Slivers" Oakley was the greatest clown of his day, a performer who could hold an audience of 8,000 people in the palm of his hand under a circus tent. He performed for the Barnum & Bailey Circus at about the time when the Marx Brothers were young men, and probably influenced the career of Harpo Marx. Slivers Oakley had one comedy routine that was famous where he played every character in a baseball game, including the players and umpire, all through pantomime, and it made whole crowds crazy with laughter.

Cool. Good to know. But what did it have to do with our friend Josh, the Class Clown of little Patton Middle School in middle-of-nowhere, Oregon?

I finally put them all together, adding Nightingales to the search, and I found out that Slivers Oakley was at the height of his fame in the early-1900s, at the same time when the Marx Brothers, who would later make the movie Horsefeathers, were performing as a singing group called the Four Nightingales.

I desperately wished that I could print this out, but printing cost a dime a page and I was busted. I had given my last quarter to Josh. As I wistfully stared at the printer, Mrs. Berg, the librarian who wins the award for Best Hair Ever (Research & Libraries Division), came up to me.

"Problem, Omar?"

"Just wish I could print something out," I said.

She slipped a quarter into the machine. "Go ahead. It's on me."

"I'll pay you back," I promised.

"I know you will," she said, and then had to fix a massive tangle of curls that had fallen over her eyes. "You

know what my dad always says? I spent $50,000 to send my son to college to play football, and all I got was a quarterback."

I think it was some kind of joke. I thanked her and returned to my computer screen. But what did it all mean? I had just received a nice lesson on clowns and vaudeville and a family named Marx in the early years of the 20th-century. But I still wasn't any closer to finding my friend Josh. And now I was getting worried, and wondered if I needed to report his disappearance. To whom? School was closed. The police, maybe. His mom and dad, certainly. I knew that the minute that happened, all heck would break loose and I might get into a lot of trouble for letting Josh go off on his own downtown on his bike.

In my life, diary, things happen. They just do. I've always counted on that. I'm not saying that they happen for some great, important, cosmic reason. I'm just saying that I've always found that if I wait long enough and look hard enough and think things through, I'll begin to understand things. Something good will happen. My whole life, I've counted on good things to happen, and then they generally do.

I gave myself the rest of the day to figure out where to look next for Josh. To let something happen, in other words. And if nothing came to me or nothing happened…well, then I would tell everyone what I knew. Or in this case, didn't know. If there was one certain thing, it was that I really didn't have any clue what had become of my good pal.

The Humor. Knowing Josh, it would turn out to be something funny. And for his sake, I desperately hoped it was.

CHAPTER FOURTEEN: THE FIFTH NIGHTINGALE

I woke up with an idea. As Dr. Seuss would say through a character who looked like an elephant with wings and a derby hat and a flowing moustache, a wonderful, fabulous, remarkable idea.

Slivers had said to text him. I knew that my friends would be looking for me and have no idea where I was. Well, texting wouldn't be invented for decades, nor did I have my phone, but from where I sat in New York City in 1908, I could see that there was plenty of text flying around. It came in the form of newspapers – there were about fifteen of them published every day in the city and they were crammed with exactly that . . . text. Pages and pages filled with stories and news items and gossip columns and adverts. And that was how I was going to communicate with my friends. Through the newspapers. I would text them the old-school way. How hard could it be to get my name in the paper in New York City of 1908?

The big clock of Ehret's Brewery, two blocks away on 93rd Street and Second Avenue, filled the window of the Marx's apartment and told us it was 7:30 a.m. There wasn't a single clock to be found in the apartment, but they didn't need one. The brewery gave them the time, both with the huge clock that they could see out of the front room of the apartment, and by the stink of beer-making that permeated the neighborhood twice a day, when the hops and barley were being cooked and made East 93rd Street smell like everyone in every apartment was burning oatmeal on their stoves at once.

I wandered into the kitchen and found the boys eating a hot cereal called kasha that Frenchie cooked up on a huge iron pot on the stove, throwing in salt and seasonings and molasses until it was just right, and then scooping mounds of it into bowls as he said, "Eat, eat!" I sat down next to Julius and Frenchie slid a bowl and spoon in front of me.

The brothers gobbled up what was in front of them, stole spoonfuls from each other's bowls and then hounded their father mercilessly for more. "Get the lead out, Pops," yelled Julius, "I've got a train to catch."

"Ja, you catch dot train to a good whacking, you vill," muttered Frenchie.

"Yeah, come on dad," chimed in little Herbert, who then lampooned his father's accent by adding, in a perfect impersonation, "you tink vee got all day? Chust make mit de grub, ja?"

Frenchie ignored him and continued to stir the pot, humming. He was a terrific cook and the kasha was delicious. I noticed that neither he nor Minnie was eating, and there was just enough to feed me and the boys.

"The theater awaits!" yelled Julius. "We've got a show coming up on Coney Island. The lights! The applause! The girls! Josh, have I mentioned the girls?"

"No, only the boys," I dead-panned.

Adolph laughed and saw that my bowl was empty, so he dumped half of his portion into my dish. "You've got to move pretty fast around here, Josh. These wolves will eat the clothes right off your back if you're not careful."

The boys cleared the dishes, Julius curled up in a corner with a book and Adolph said, "Josh, want to walk the boys to school with me?"

"Sure," I said. "Is it the same school that you went to?"

Adolph shook his head sadly. "I never made it out of the second grade," he said. "Two Irish kids threw me out the window of P.S. 86 when the teacher wasn't looking, and I never went back."

I stared at him. Adolph was dead serious. "They threw you out the *window*?" I said.

"Yah," Adolph said with a sheepish grin. "Twice. Lucky for me the window was on the first floor or I could have really been hurt. I was so little, and the two brothers were picking on me. When the teacher wasn't looking, they picked me right up and threw me out the window. When I went back in the teacher thought I was messing around, so she walloped *me* with a ruler. I still have the scars on my knuckles. Said she'd have me whipped with a hickory switch if I ever did anything like that again. Can you imagine? And ten minutes later, when she left the room to get something, those Irish boys did it again. Picked me up and threw me out the window.

"That time I didn't go back in, and in fact, I never went back to school after that. I was seven years old. I learned to read from Julius and I learned to count and handle numbers from Lenny. He taught me music, too, after Minnie paid for his piano lessons. What else do I need?"

I just shook my head. The good old days of 1908 didn't appear to be so great to me. The apartment was cold and smelly, the lightbulbs hung from wires in the ceiling and didn't work half the time, the only refrigeration was from a block of ice that they had to haul up the steps and keep in an icebox until it melted away, and the water that came out of the tap and fell into an ugly, cement sink was brown and nasty.

I reached into my shirt and pulled out my grouch bag again. The twenty-dollar bill and Omar's quarter were still in there, so I zipped it up and stuffed it back inside my shirt.

Leonard came in, looking very much like a man who had spent the entire night out gambling, shooting pool and talking people named Nunzio out of throwing him into the Harlem River. Minnie was in the living room, chatting with some relatives whom I hadn't met. Lenny looked around, and when I caught his eye, I asked if I could speak with him in the bedroom.

"That's funny, I was going to ask you the same thing," he said. "Can we talk?"

"Be careful, Josh," called out Julius. "The last person who answered yes to that question had his fingers broken by the bookies on 95th Street."

"They were the totally unnecessary fingers," shot back Leonard. "Didn't even miss 'em. And you don't know nothing. It wasn't the bookies, it was the touts on 79th Street."

"Sorry, my mistake," said Julius, "I tout differently."

Leonard took me into the bedroom and closed the door. He leaned against the wall, and for a weird moment, just stood there looking at me, as if he were sizing me up. Grandfather said that Chico was the smartest and the shrewdest of the Marx Brothers, the older brother who guided their careers and made all of the movie deals. Now he was looking at me as if I were a hand of poker and he was trying to figure out the best way to play it.

"So I heard that you think the Marx Brothers should be a comedy act," he said slowly.

I gulped. I wasn't so sure anymore why I was there or what I was supposed to do. I nodded.

"All I know is that where I come from, you are…or were…a comedy act. One of the funniest comedy acts ever."

He nodded. "I agree. I've always thought the same thing. But Minnie needs some convincing. She's scared to change things. And now I'm gonna tell you two things, Josh. You listen carefully."

He walked up to me and put his hands on my shoulders and looked me right in the eye. "The first one is, you do what you have to do to stay strong and stay alive," he said. "Whatever it takes. The second thing is never give up, or fall into despair. Everything's gonna work out great. Got it?"

I had no idea what he was talking about. "Um, sure."

I was a little floored by that. I had never seen a Marx Brother be so serious.

"Now what did you want to ask me?" he said.

"I've got an idea," I said. "I want you to get me onto the billing for the show on Sunday. I want to be one of the Four Nightingales. And it's very important that you get my name into the newspapers saying I'm part of the act. Josh Markowitz. Make sure they use my whole name.

His eyebrows shot up and he looked at me again as if he were trying to figure out what or who in the world I really was.

"Get your name into the papers. Like you're a nightingale."

"Yep."

He shook his head. "That's really strange, Josh. Because I was thinking exactly the same thing. Come with me."

I followed him out to the living room, where he walked up to Minnie and tapped her on the shoulder. "Minnie, Mrs. Levy asked me to give this to you," he said, taking an envelope from the pocket of his jacket and handing it to her. She tore it open, pulled out a card inside, read it and then frowned.

"Lou Levy is very sick, and can't perform this week," she said. "Lennie, you're going to have to take his place." Lou Levy, I remembered, was the fourth member of their singing act, the Four Nightingales. The other three were Julius, Adolph and Milton. Family lore had it that the first time that Adolph was pulled into the act, at a dinner theater on Coney Island, he wet his pants on stage from sheer stage fright.

"Oh, no, don't look at me," Leonard said. "The horses are running on Sunday. I've got a better idea." He cast a long look at me. "Hey, Josh," he said, "can you sing?"

Julius looked up from his book and then jumped to his feet and stood on the couch. "Can he sing? Can he SING? Why, this boy can sing like an angel. Look at the little cherub. Look at his rosy cheeks. Why, he'll have the audience eating out of his hand. And if he's not careful they'll eat the hand, too. Can he sing? Why, this is the voice that has launched a thousand ships. Or at least a couple of sailboats at Central Park."

"Ah, you're a little dinghy," Leonard shot back.

Julius sat down just as abruptly as he had stood up, and picked up his book. "Maybe so. Well, Josh," he said after a minute, "can you sing?"

"Of course he can sing," Leonard said quickly. "Everybody can sing. I'll teach him everything he needs to know. We've got four days to teach him. Piece of cake. Ladies and gentlemen," he said, clapping me on the back, "I give to you the Fifth Nightingale!"

Into my ear he whispered, "Don't worry about nothing. I'm gonna take good care of you."

CHAPTER FIFTEEN: FROM THE DIARY OF ELIZABETH WALCOT WOOLCOTT

Dearest, Darling, Delicious (and thus, Delightful) Diary,
This is one of the reasons why I wanted to come to America in the first place. Marvelous things seem to happen here ALL the time. Maybe not quite as marvelous as a steak and kidney pie in the Harrod's food court. But dashed near as marvelous. One need only pop down to the local Wendy's and experience the miracle that is a chocolate Frosty to appreciate American marvelousness at its most marvelous. One time I ate five of them at one sitting just to truly appreciate the true miracle of the Frosty.
So today Omar rang up the house in search of Mistress Amy, who was so terribly wrapped up in the lives of the Kardashians that I'm afraid she didn't have a moment to devote to good old Mr. O. But I did, so I agreed to meet him downtown at the old Serendipity ice-cream parlor. As you know, diary, I have quite gotten over the awful, horrible experience of waiting for a certain Mr. Josh M. at the very same ice-cream shop only days before. Mr.

O. seemed quite urgently desiring to meet up, so I buckled up the old patent-leathers and biffled down to Third Street (or rue Troisieme, as our French friends might drolly put it).

Well, Omar's knickers were all a-twist over some new information he had learned in The Mysterious Case of the Missing Markowitz. At first he went on and on about Googling the Horsefeathers and Marx Brothers and all kinds of assorted and quite boring historical fluffenstuff. But then he got to the meat of it.

"One more thing finally occurred to me," he said (and here, diary, I am quoting). "It always does, you know. I went back to the library and just for the heck of it, I added the name Josh Markowitz to the string of search terms I had used before. And it all came together. An old newspaper clipping came up from something called the New York Standard that said in April of 1908, at a theater on Coney Island in New York City, a singing group called the Four Nightingales was performing. Three of the singers listed in the cast were named Julius Marx, Adolph Marx, and Milton Marx. The fourth singer listed on the program was named Josh Markowitz."

Alas and alack, dear diary, our loveable Class Clown had somehow, and for some reason that I can't quite fathom, managed to go back in time.

Not to tell jokes and be funny, but to sing with the lads who would one day become The Marx Brothers. As all of the eighth grade wits at Patton Middle School drolly put it, Go figure.

That's where we would find our friend, Josh. That's where he was. How we were going to find him continued to be a complete and utter mystery. I looked at Omar. He looked at me.

"Weird," we both said at once, and then stared off into space for a good long while. I think he likes Amy more than moi.

"I've got an idea," I said. "We've got to get in touch with Slivers the Clown. He's the last one to see Josh, and he might be the only one on Earth who knows how to find him. And bring him back."

Omar agreed, I paid for the ice-cream, and after sharing a scoop or three of the old pistachio, we screwed our courage up to the breaking point and went back down to the warehouse to give The Great Wandini a good biffing about. But only after looking in every nook and cranny of the place, hoping to find the clown, Slivers, with no luck.

We approached The G.W. and asked it where we might find Slivers, but the only response we got was the tiniest bit of paper that merely said, "Text him." And then The G.W. went dark and couldn't be started up again.

"I don't even own a phone," Omar admitted. "My family can't afford it." He looked so sad and a little embarrassed and I felt so absolutely, frightfully bad for him that I wished I could have just given him my Samsung Galaxy Infinity on the spot and knicker off to the market to buy another one for myself. Which would make my father, I mean Uncle Milton, quite horribly furious.

"It doesn't matter," Omar pointed out. "We still wouldn't be able to text the clown. We don't have his number."

Well, the two of us were positively hornswoggled over this, and I admit, diary, that I also entertained some dark thoughts about ever being able to help our friend Josh, who appeared to be stuck in the past, like the people who only listen to the oldies radio station and watch old sitcoms on Nickelodeon all day long. One of those ancient sitcoms being The Patty Duke Show, about identical cousins, one from America, one from England, who look and talk and walk alike, and honestly, I don't quite see the point and prefer to watch The Partridge Family.

But I got to thinking about it, rather intensively. How would you text someone eighty-odd years before texting was even invented? What could this possibly mean, dear D.? Was the Great Wandini having a wally on all of us?

Well pish-posh to that, I said to myself. No fortune-teller is going to make a monkey out of Elizabeth Walcot Woolcott. With Master Omar in tow, I began to search the warehouse, past the Great Wandini, which was now quite dark and sinister, even if he did look like Vice-President Joe Biden, and past the quite terrifying head of Bobo the Ape that sat on a shelf. I wasn't quite sure what I was looking for, but then it became apparent when I saw it. In a corner, and partially hidden under a sheet, was an old typesetting apparatus.   And lying before us, in metal type, was the mocked-up front page of the New York Standard newspaper. It was dated April 17, 1908, and on the side of the page, under Franklin Pierce Adams' column, was a large, white space that contained three words.

Insert Text Here.

So I did. I found the metal letters I needed, and spelled out these words in the blank space: SLIVERS, JOSH NEEDS YOU.

I stood back, wondering what, if anything, to do next. I will admit to feeling a little lost, and a little daft. As if I had gone to Picadilly Circus or Hyde Park, let's say, without my wellies, on a rainy London day. It rather reminded me of the first time I went underground to ride the tube by myself and got quite astonishingly lost somewhere in the vicinity of Notting Hill.

But then, diary, before my astonished eyes, the type on the page seemed to slowly vanish, like when you shake an Etch-a-Sketch, and then rearrange itself into these words.

WHERE IS JOSH?

"On Coney Island!" Omar blurted out. "He's going to be singing on Coney Island in three days. Tell him!"

So I found the letters and inserted them into the box.

HENDERSON'S BEER GARDEN. CONEY ISLAND ON SUNDAY. FIND JOSH. SEND HIM HOME.

We waited five minutes. Then ten. Then another ten. It was getting dark and especially terrifying in the magic shop, and thoughts of Jack the Ripper danced merrily in my head. We were about to leave when the words on the page blurred and one last thing came up.

JOSH WHO?

Omar looked at me. I looked at him. We shook our heads. "Clowns," he said with more than a trace of disgust in his voice.

Clowns, I repeat. Too bloody funny, dear diary, for their own good sometimes.

CHAPTER SIXTEEN: UP THE RIVER

A few minutes later, I went out to the sidewalk to meet up with Adolph and walk the boys to school, but they weren't there. As I looked around, Leonard came out of a doorway and walked up to me. He patted me on the back and said again, "Remember, everything's gonna work out great." And then he raised two fingers to his lips and let out a loud whistle.

Three men came out of the doorway and walked over to us. Two of them wore dark suits; I had never seen them before. The third was wearing the big hat and the blue uniform and badge of the New York Police Department. I had definitely seen him before. Stitched in gold lettering over the pocket of the shirt was the officer's name: Mulcahy. The four of them surrounded us so there was no escaping them.

"Alright, ya little gypsy, you're coming with us," said the officer, grabbing me by the arm and squeezing it so tightly that I didn't dare move.

"I didn't DO anything!" I yelled. "Where are you taking me?"

"We've got a place where little street rats like you can do some good for the world. We found a nice job for ya, upstate in the mills."

"No!" I yelled again. I was terrified. "You can't take me there. You have no right! I want to speak to a lawyer!"

Mulcahy brandished his heavy nightstick and threatened to hit me with it. "I've got all the right I need right here, and I'll use it if you don't come along peaceful."

"Leonard, help!" I pleaded. But Lenny Marx barely glanced at me. He was standing beside the two men in dark suits, and as I watched, one of the men handed him a dollar. "Nice work, genius," said the man. "Here's your finder's fee."

"Pleasure doing business," said Leonard. He grabbed the bill from the man's fingers and stuffed it into his pocket. Mulcahy roughly pulled on my arm and we started walking down the street.

"Hey, wait a second, there's one more thing," Leonard called out.

He walked up to me and without another word, reached his hand inside my suit coat, and then inside my shirt. He found what he was looking for under the shirt, against my skin. He yanked so hard on the grouch bag that the cord that held it around my neck snapped, leaving an angry red mark on my skin.

"Won't be needing this where you're going," said Leonard, stuffing the bag into his own pocket. "I'll take good care of it. See you in the future, Josh. Don't take any wooden nickels."

He calmly turned around and walked back into the apartment building.

I almost started to cry, not only because I was scared but because I was so angry at Leonard "Chico" Marx. How could he do this to me? I had no idea where we were going, but I did know that my chances of ever getting home again fell to almost zero if I left New York City.

Mulcahy dragged me down the street. When we turned the corner onto Third Avenue, a small crowd, mostly kids, was waiting for us. They had seen the officer and the textile agents, and they knew that a kid would be leaving the neighborhood with them. Every child on the Upper East Side of New York worried at some point in his life that it might be himself, a brother, a friend who was dragged off to work upstate in the mills. It came as a collective relief to see another boy get taken. A boy that none of them had ever seen before.

They laughed and jeered at me as Mulcahy led me down the street. They threw rotten tomatoes and fruit at me, splattering my new suit coat and pants. As we neared the corner of Lexington Avenue, a boy ran up to me and shoved something hard, made out of paper, onto my head.

It was a red-and-white dunce cap, just like the one that Mr. Yanuzzi displayed in his office. The other kids all howled with laughter, and threw things at me, the dunce, until I was pushed into the back of a horse-drawn paddy wagon. Mulcahy slammed the door shut behind me and locked it. The wagon was bare wood inside, with only a long bench to sit on, and two windows with bars that I could barely see out of if I stood on the bench.

The wagon rolled. There were ten sharp bangs of sound as rocks were thrown at the side of the wagon, and then only the sounds and sights and smells of New York City rolling by as I began the long journey upstate to an uncertain, but sure to be horrible future in the textile mills. I vaguely remembered reading something in history class about America's Industrial Revolution. I had no desire to experience it first-hand, but here I was, about to become a worker in the great machine of our country's phenomenal growth. A growth that would allow kids to not have to go to work and have free public schools by the year 2012.

Which is where I desperately wanted to be at the moment.

CHAPTER SEVENTEEN: FROM THE DIARY OF STEVIE SAN PEDRO

Beer Diary,
*   There is a perfectly good reason why I left that stupid warehouse downtown when the other kids were looking for Markoworst and some weird, old clown.*
*   I suddenly remembered an important appointment. And I wanted to get my homework done early so I could take the rest of spring break off without worrying about it. It was for extra credit, and unlike some kids at Patton Middle School, such as the ones named Omar and Amy, I care about my academic record. See, I don't live in the past like some people (named Josh). I am always looking towards my bright, secure future.*
*   The other reason was that it was creepy down there at the warehouse. There, I said it. Happy, Deer Diary? And as you of all diaries may recall, getting scared and being placed in creepy situations makes me break out in a full-body rash. Which has been proven how many times at Halloween? Do we really have to go through that again? The terror, the screaming, the running home in tears, the pants-wetting, the awful itching? Anyone need to see that again? I didn't think so. My mom says to avoid*

frightening situations that might make me break out, and she's only a public health official with a Masters degree in Third World rashes, so why should anyone listen to her?

Now they're telling me that Markowit-less is, like, stuck in the past or something.

As if.

As frickety if.

Like I'm supposed to believe that? Is there a single person in this school besides me with a brain in their head?

Everybody who knows even the slightest thing about time travel knows that you don't get stuck in the past. Hello! Watch every single movie ever made about time travel and the guy always manages to return to his own time. They go back to their own time, and then the movie is over. I rest my case.

If Birdbrain Markowitz is really stuck in the past, I hope he'll be smart enough to buy Microsoft and Amazon stock. Or bet all of his money on the 1927 Yankees. What an idiot. But he's a lucky idiot. I'm sure he'll figure out a way to slip on a puddle in the past or something that turns out to be the black hole that brings him right back here. And then he'll be all like, "I'm back! Did I miss anything? Can I copy your extra-credit notes?"

And I'll probably let him. Why? Because maybe then I'll be able to figure out why Amy/Elizabeth – who, HELLO! are the same person!! – even likes him. What's to like? I don't get it.

At least I think they're the same person. I've never seen them together in the same room. So that proves it, right?

Why am I even asking you? You're just a stupid diary.

One more thing. I'm thinking of calling Elizabeth Walcot Woolcott. I mean, since MarkoWishes is away, and he stood her up anyway, why shouldn't I ask her out? WHAT DOES HE HAVE THAT I HAVEN'T GOT??!

Uh oh, I feel an itch coming on. Mom? MOM!! Get the lotion.

CHAPTER EIGHTEEN: PADDY WAGON

I spent the rest of that day and that night in the paddy wagon, with only the clothes Frenchie had given me to keep warm. I ripped open the seam of the dunce cap and flattened the cardboard out to use as a bed to lay on, and used the suit jacket as a blanket. Sometime in the evening, just after dusk, Mulcahy opened the door and threw me a piece of rock-hard bread and a chunk of moldy cheese, and that was the only food or human contact I had since the mob splattered me with rotten tomatoes, bits of which I picked off my clothing and ate.

Delicious, I said to myself, imagining I was at a French restaurant with my beautiful English date, Elizabeth Walcot Woolcott. Would *monsieur* like some champagne to go with the rotten tomato bits? But, of course. Would Madame care for a tiny, little palate cleanser? Just a spoonful? A savory little morsel? What's that, *madame*, you ask is it posh? Oh, absolutely, miss, no expense was spared to *amuse* your *bouche*. It's the poshest of the posh. You might say it's rather posh-isimo. Rather.

I imagined the whole dinner, right down to dessert and the exquisite strings of red licorice that I ate from one end and she from the other, Lady and the Tramp-style. "Oh, I say!" she exclaimed when our lips met.

"So do I," I murmured back, snatching the last of the licorice for myself with a deft movement of the tongue.

"Good show, Jawsh!"

I amused myself this way for most of the day, taking breaks from my imaginary date with Elizabeth to stand on the bench and watch the landscape pass out the window. That, and imagining the precise angle and speed of delivery with which I'd kick Leonard "Chico" Marx in the family jewels if I ever saw him again.

We were somewhere in the country when the door opened the next morning. I stirred from the floor, half asleep, and Mulcahy grabbed me and threw me out of the wagon and onto the ground. I lay there a moment, smelling fresh grass and feeling cold, wet dew on my cheek. We were out of the city and in the country. It smelled fresher, less polluted – kind of like Oregon. I was given a small glass bottle of milk, which I drank in one long, desperate swallow, and then Mulcahy handed me a small loaf of dark bread that I tore into, gobbling it down before it could be taken away. If there was one thing I had learned about living in 1908 for the last three days, it was to not take anything for granted.

"Where are you taking me?" I asked in my bravest voice. "I didn't do anything. I want to talk to a lawyer at once. My parents are very rich and important and you'll get in trouble for this."

"Aw, shut up, you, shut yer yap," was the only response that I got.

Midway through the day I was transferred to another wagon that was drawn by a huge, Belgian draft horse. I was grateful because it was an open wagon, and I got to sit on the front bench, albeit handcuffed to the railing, next to a man with an enormous, overflowing moustache who spat tobacco, drove the horse and didn't so much as look at me for the entire day. Mulcahy left that morning after receiving his own payoff from the factory agents in suits, one of whom rode along in the back of the wagon, sleeping most of the time on bales of hay. He also didn't say a word to me.

It was a warm day, and I stopped shivering as the wagon bumped north to the village of Sleepy Hollow, and then rolled onto a flat ferryboat that crossed the Hudson River by way of stout cords that had been stretched across the water. When I told the driver that I had to pee, the man just looked at me, spat tobacco onto my shoes and looked away, so I relieved myself by unbuttoning the trousers with one hand, contorting my body sideways and peeing off the side of the wagon as it rolled and creaked along.

I had time to think about everything that had happened to me, all the way back to my meeting with Mr. Yanuzzi in his dungeon torture chamber. And then going to see crazy, old Slivers the Clown. In what possible misguided comic dimension would someone who was trying to entertain people call himself *Slivers*?

And how could it be that I was singled out to do this thing for the Marx Brothers? Turn them away from singing and launch their comedy careers.

I mean, seriously?

I mean, are you totally kidding me?

I'm just a kid, and there must have been some mistake. If that's the case, am I stuck in 1908 because of a decrepit, senile clown's accident?! A case of mistaken identity by an old man who smears paste makeup all over his face and thinks that George W. Bush is still the president?

The driver looked over at me and spat more tobacco juice on my shoes. I realized that I had been talking out loud. "Thank you sir, may I have another?" I said. The driver ignored me and drove on.

We camped that night in a heavily wooded area. I was allowed to lie in the back of the wagon in the hay, but only after I was handcuffed to a heavy, iron ring imbedded in the floor of the wagon. It was so uncomfortable that I barely slept. I admit that I cried for my mom and dad in the middle of the night, but then I thought of what Leonard Marx told me before selling me to the factory agents. "Don't give up, don't despair."

Easy for him to say.

It took nearly all of the third day to complete the trip to the complex of textile factories that made up the Oneida Mills company, on the south bank of the Mohawk River. The wagon stopped twice for food at farmhouses, but I was handcuffed to it the whole time, and the driver and factory agent only brought me scraps of food to eat, and about two cups of water to drink all day. As we got farther north, the air changed from sweet-smelling to foul again, like the city had smelled. It was the factory. I could smell it before we even got there and saw smoke belching out of a tall chimney of one of the buildings.

The wagon entered a fenced compound and pulled up to a wooden dormitory building around ten o'clock that night. It was quiet and dark, and a man with a lantern came out to talk to the driver. The factory agent finally roused himself from his deep, carefree sleep, unlocked my handcuffs and then handed me over to the man with the lantern. Money was exchanged, and without another word, the factory agent and tobacco-spitting driver turned the wagon around and clomped off into the night.

"Come with me," said the man with the lantern, "and don't try anything stupid. We're miles and miles away from anything even resembling civilization."

I looked closer and realized that it wasn't a man at all, but a kid of maybe twelve years old, tall and hefty for his age. I followed him into the dormitory and, as soon as we set foot inside, I was greeted by the smells and snoring of 150 filthy boys sleeping two to a mattress on bunkbeds. The profound, deeply unsettling odor of unwashed feet nearly knocked me flat.

"Here's the new kid," said the guy with the lantern. He was talking to another boy, a little older, maybe fifteen. "Name's Markowitz. Josh Markowitz."

The older boy walked up and stood right in front of me. He looked me up and down. "What kind of a stupid name is that?" he snarled. And then he stepped forward and punched me in the stomach, hard enough to make me sink to my knees, gagging, trying to remember how to breathe.

Nobody had ever hit me like that before. I have never even been in a fight. Smacking people, especially strangers, is typically frowned upon in the 21st century.

"From now on, your name is Jerry," said the older boy. "Jerry Lewis. Now go get some sleep. Tomorrow morning you're going straight to hell."

If you think that maybe I had had a rough couple of days since I was kidnapped outside of the Marx's apartment, you can think again. That wagon ride and punch in the stomach were actually the nicest things that would happen to me during the time I was forced into labor at the Oneida Mills Company.

CHAPTER NINETEEN: DAISY

"His name is Daisy. He punches every new kid in the stomach. Don't feel bad."

"His real name is Oliver Maxwell, Jr."

"But everyone calls him Daisy. He gives a new name to every kid."

"Jerry Lewis isn't such a bad name. He named one kid Ignatz Stromboli."

"His uncle owns the factory."

"He's a total jackass."

"Be careful with that bucket. The last kid who carried that stuff spilled some on himself."

"They found him twitching on the floor with yellow foam coming out of his mouth."

"I think he died. You got his job."

"Oh crap, here comes Daisy. Clam up, already."

These conversations, or snippets of conversation, took place over the next two days in the mill between me and two other boys who passed by me every few hours as they did their jobs. They only dared to say a sentence or two before moving on. Their names were Leslie and Harry. They were both eight years old, orphans, and had been working in the mill since they were five. Nobody else spoke to me.

After my punch-in-the-stomach greeting from the boy called Daisy, I found an empty cot in the back of the dormitory, deep within the stink of feet, and fell asleep exhausted, hungry and terrified. I woke up at five-thirty a.m. to the sharp thwack of a stick hitting the iron frames of the cots, and the howls of pain from boys who didn't wake up fast enough and received the thwack of the stick on the soles of their exposed feet. Daisy ran a tight ship.

We shuffled outside in the cold, damp morning, lined up alongside the river and peed, and then pooped into buckets, using scraps of cloth to wipe ourselves. The cloth was remnants of fabric that we made in the factory in a new process called corduroy, and it was rough and scratchy and tore at our skin. Some of the boys threw their soiled scraps of cloth into the buckets, some threw them on the ground and some rinsed them out in the river and shoved them in their pockets to use again later.

It was the new boy's job to clean up the buckets and the scraps of cloth. "Jerry Lewis!" barked Daisy, "dump the buckets in the river, wash them and bring them back to the dormitory. And hurry up if you expect to have breakfast."

I only threw up twice getting all of the buckets cleaned and rinsed out in the river, and the cloths picked up. I pretty much stank and was filthy when I brought the last of the rinsed buckets back to the dorm and piled them in a corner, but there was no place to wash. There was a bowl of thin oatmeal and a cup of milk waiting for me at the long table where all of the boys ate, but I could see from the smudges on the bowl that boys had dipped their fingers into my food to sneak an extra bite for themselves. I closed my eyes and ate the oatmeal anyway without looking at it, but then the thought of all of those filthy fingers dipping into my food made me go outside and throw it up. Rating my day so far on a scale of one to ten, I'd say I was at negative infinity.

Daisy wasn't much older than me, but he was a head taller and as broad through the shoulders as a man. He was in charge of making sure the boys worked hard and followed the rules, and he did his job with an efficient, violent fury. Escape was nearly impossible. I could see adult guards posted at the edges of the mill property, which was surrounded by a tall fence to make sure that no boys made a run for it.

And where would they go even if they could slip out unnoticed? We were dozens of miles away from other towns in the woods and forests of upstate New York. Most of the boys conscripted to work there had come from orphanages that were too full to keep them. With no money, no parents or family to look after them, most of them would never leave the mill.

Harry and Les could have been brothers, with their dark, black hair, skinny bodies and big, brown eyes. They remembered almost nothing about their lives before the mill, and their families, only that they had been delivered upstate as little kids. They had worked their way up to be doffers, the boys who climbed high up on the mill machines and removed spindles of thread that had been spun and collected, wrestling the heavy spindles off of the spinner while it was still moving, and replacing them with blank spindles.

Neither one of them had pinkie fingers on their right hands. Most of the other doffers didn't, either.

"It got caught in the spindle."

"You should have seen the blood."

"Daisy beat me for a week after it happened. Said I should be more careful. You shoulda seen what he done to Les."

"They never did find my finger."

"You don't look so good. Have you been breathing in the dyes?"

"Don't ever breathe in the dyes."

Daisy put me to work in the dye department, filling buckets with chemicals that were siphoned out of wooden kegs. Three sallow, ashen-faced men instructed me on which chemicals to put into the buckets. I thought the men were about fifty years old. They were actually boys of fifteen.

Some of the dyes were pigments that stank like turpentine or acetone. Others were acids that sizzled and smoked when I poured them into the buckets, and burned holes through my clothes if the tiniest drops splashed up. The worst ones were mordants, or chemicals that stabilized the colors once they were introduced to fabrics. They smelled like pure evil, like rat poison mixed with the stuff that unclogs drains. I would carry the buckets across the football field-sized factory floor to the boilers and pour them into a funnel, where they would bubble and fizz and release a cloud of noxious odors that burned my nose and lungs. The floor was wet and slippery and I soon found that, like the other boys, I was less likely to slip if I was barefoot, even though it meant stepping in chemicals and wastewater from the dyeing process.

The boys worked from six-thirty in the morning until noon, and then were given a thirty-minute break for lunch of soup and bread, which we ate together in silence at long, wooden tables. There was no talking allowed. Daisy saw to that, marching up and down behind the benches where the boys sat, making sure we didn't steal each other's food or speak. Things loosened up a little bit after we were done. A boy would pull out a ball made from scraps of corduroy cloth that he had wadded up and sealed with candle wax, and some of the boys would throw the ball and run around until the whistle blew to go back to work.

I never participated in those games. I was too tired all of the time, and the chemicals made me feel sick.

We worked until seven, lined up at a single water spigot to quickly wash our hands and faces, and then headed back to the dorm for a required prayer, light supper and bedtime at eight.

"Who are we praying to?"

"The Good Lord."

"If he's so good, why are we working in this factory like slaves and crapping in buckets?"

"Shut up! You want Daisy to hear you? You don't know how good you have it now if you get on his bad side."

"Just shut up and pray."

"Yeah. Some people in the world don't even *have* buckets."

I was so exhausted that I passed out the minute I lay down at night on the rough cot, with a mattress that was a filthy burlap cloth stuffed with straw and lumpy bits of cloth remnants. It was good that I was so tired, because then I didn't feel the bedbugs and lice that came out every night and bit big, red welts into my legs and arms, which itched horribly during the day.

"Be careful around Daisy. He's nuts."

"Have a joke ready if he asks you. He always asks the new kid to tell him a joke."

"If he doesn't like it, you'll get the bread with worms in it."

"And he has no sense of humor. He hasn't liked a joke yet."

"Be more careful where you walk. Your feet are starting to bleed."

"The skin rubs off if you walk in the wrong puddles."

Daisy left me alone after the first night's brutal introduction, but on the third day, as I was wearily trudging back to the dorm, he was waiting for me. He grabbed me by the arm and shoved me against a wall.

"You look like a funny guy, Jerry Lewis," he sneered. "A regular class clown. So tell me a joke, clown. Make me laugh."

I never knew this before, but it's hard to be funny and think of jokes when you're afraid that someone is about to punch you in the stomach and knock the wind out of you. I was drawing a total blank in the joke-telling department.

Daisy grabbed my arm and twisted it behind my back so hard that I thought it was going to break.

"Okay, look," I said, grimacing in pain. "I was hunting in Africa and one night I killed an elephant in my pajamas. How he got into my pajamas, I'll never know."

Daisy released my arm and something resembling a thought seemed to pass over his face. Then he shoved me face first into the wall, but not hard enough to really hurt me. "That's the stupidest joke I ever heard. Like how was the elephant supposed to fit in your pajamas?"

He stalked away. But that night at dinner, my bread didn't have worms crawling through it.

I'll count that as comic relief. There was a little countdown clock in my head that got louder and louder. It was counting down the days left that Slivers had told me I must get my job done, or risk never returning to my own time. And every day and night that I spent in that horrid factory made the clock even louder, telling me that I would never get out of there and was stuck forever. How would that make my Mom and Dad feel, that I never returned from spring break? Or would I never have existed at all, if my whole life played out in an awful factory in 1908 New York? Would never be born, never knew my folks or friends, never told a single joke in my Class Clown life?

Terrible thoughts. And I had plenty of time to think about them as the clock ticked on.

CHAPTER TWENTY: FROM THE DIARY OF ELIZABETH WALCOT WOOLCOTT

Best. Day. Ever.

And yes, I am counting the time that we went to the Tower of London and Dad pretended to steal the Crown Jewels and we had such a frightful time before the magistrate, convincing him that it was just a joke and Dad didn't actually swallow the Koh-i-Noor diamond and attempt to smuggle it out of the tower in his stomach, and they let him go with a severe reprimand, and we wound up eating bangers & mash at the local pub while Dad roared with laughter and the lads roared things back at him that were incomprehensible because they were Cockneys, not from posh Kensington like us.

And wouldn't you know it, this time the fun came as an utter surprise, which is another thing I adore about America – anything goes here, and everyone has the chance to redeem him or herself.

I'm referring of course to Steven San Pedro, who rang me up, and after much hemming and hawing about, asked me to meet him downtown. Seems he still didn't believe us about Josh going back through time and wanted to have his own look at Slivers' Magic Shop, but was reluctant to do so by himself owing to a mysterious skin condition that sounds positively beastly and rare.

Could I meet him? I'd be delighted, I replied, and rang off.

Well, I made my excuses at home with Amy, who was jazzercising, and toddled off to the other side of town, where I purchased two delicious tamales from the Al Paraiso food truck and washed them down with the gallon-sized Slurpee in assorted tropical flavors from the Circle K store as part of my intensive research into the eating habits of American pre-teenagers.

I was thus quite full and satisfied when I reached Slivers' Magic Shop, and found Steven San Pedro cowering behind a bush, where he rather unconvincingly explained that he was conducting research on urban landscaping and often turned this particular shade of white shortly before the itching commenced.

Whatever, dear Diary, as the 7th-grade girls at Patton Middle School are prone to repeat every four minutes or so. Whatever.

We went inside and after much coaxing, I led Steven to the back of the store where the Great Wandini sat, and explained to him that we thought that the magician, with the help of Slivers the Clown, had somehow managed to send Josh back in time.

Well, that's ridiculous, announced Master San Pedro in the voice that he uses in pre-algebra class that invariably gets the answer right but makes the rest of the class hate him. A voice that has been compared to a whining baby whose diaper needs to be changed, but I feel that is uncharitable. I know several lads in England with far whinier voices whose skin breaks out with much less provocation.

Watch, he said, I'm grasping the magician's hand and nothing is happening. Am I going back in time? Are you?

Well, no, I admitted, but then we noticed something. At the back of the Great Wandini box was a little slot, nearly hidden by a molding of wood, and when with considerable effort we picked up the corner and looked under it, we discovered a small compartment. Steven – oh dear, resourceful Steven – pulled out a screwdriver that he kept on his person for protection, and in short order he had opened the compartment and out spilled two shiny tokens of a style and origin that we had never before seen.

I won't go into the ensuing multiple attempts that Steven made to leave the premises, or the fount of strength that I summoned to drag him back from the door. Suffice it to say that it took some coaxing to get him to get on with it.

But get on with it he did. He inserted the two tokens into the slot, grasped the Great Wandini's hand with one of his own, and then quite manfully grasped my hand, too.

Where to? he asked.

I don't know, I said, I guess if I could go anywhere I'd like to go to London and see the world premiere of a Gilbert & Sullivan operetta.

Sure, like I really know what that is, he said, I was thinking more along the lines of we'd go into the future and find out how to cure rashes. But fine. He muttered something to the Great Wandini, who had lit up and was making quite astonishing grunting and time-travel-esque noises.

Poof! We suddenly found ourselves sitting in the orchestra section of the Savoy Theater, which, as you know, diary, is my favorite theater in the entire world, owing to it being off the charts in the posh category.

It was 1882, Steven was suddenly wearing a tuxedo and a monocle, and I a smashing ballgown, and with unbridled delight we watched the first-ever production of Iolanthe. *It was sensational. The fairies were a delight, and the Lord Chancellor magnificent. I've never had a better time at the theater.*

Alright, so maybe Steven scratched a bit more than one might wish in an escort, and whimpered frequently about needing to get back to do his homework.

When the show concluded and the cast finished their bows to thunderous applause and a standing ovation from everyone save one white and trembling lad who remained cowering in his seat, poof! we were transported back to Slivers' shop. It was exactly one minute later on my watch than when we left, but I swear, diary, we had been away for hours. Simply hours.

And then Steven and I looked at each other with what the French call amour in our eyes. I took a step closer to him. He took a step closer to me.

Well, then he fainted dead away onto the floor. But was quickly revived by a series of small, strategically placed slaps to the cheek and jaw areas.

He was so sweet when he came to, clinging to me like a koala bear and calling for his mommy. That's when I really fell hard, dear diary. I don't know how to tell Josh this when and if he ever gets back, but I've found a new beau. Now we're thinking about using the Great Wandini to catch an original Shakespeare play – a comedy, of course – at the Old Globe.

But only after Steven's itching subsides and the swelling goes down. He said, as he hastily bid adieu, that he would call me "when the coast was clear." Not sure why we'd bring the coast into this, but fine, I said, my true love, adieu, adieu.

He fell over on his bike, got back on, and sped away like the wind.

Oh well, Josh has been gone for four days now, and a girl my age mustn't expect to wait forever. I hope we'll always stay friends, if he ever comes back. Judging from Slivers' ability to track anything for more than two minutes, it seems like even money that Josh may be stuck in 1908 forever. Oh well, I hope he has a good life in the past. We will miss him at Patton Middle School graduation and promotion to the 8th grade day.

I repeat. Best. Day. Ever.

Ta-ta for now from your faithful correspondent, Elizabeth. Walcot. Woolcott.

CHAPTER TWENTY-ONE: THE AFRICAN EXPLORER

There was a buzz in the factory the next day. The boys were excited about something, and it took most of the morning for me to piece together what was happening. At first I thought that my elephant joke was being spread around, the pathetic curse of the comic, always hoping for a laugh, but then, after passing Harry and Les a half-dozen times, I figured out that a VIP was coming to the factory.

"Super rich guy."
"Big game hunter."
"Coming today."
"The African explorer."
"Wants to order a massive amount of corduroy."
"All the way from Africa."
"Needs a boy to go back with him."
"Needs a boy to take to Africa."
"Wants to make a boy his son and take him out of here."
"All the way to Africa."

"And doesn't care if the boy has all his fingers."

At seven o'clock, just before the whistle blew to end the work day and it was so dark in the factory that I had to find my way from the chemical room to the boilers by feel, not by sight, I heard something that I hadn't heard all week.

Silence. The big machines had stopped for the first time. The room was still.

In the gathering darkness, I saw what appeared to be five men standing in the corner of the boiler room. I got closer, carefully setting the buckets down in order to avoid a shower of burning acid drops. I made out the figures of Daisy and an older man who must have been Daisy's uncle, the owner of the factory.

They were talking with three men who gave every appearance of having just arrived from Africa. Two of them were natives. They wore only loincloths. I couldn't be sure from where I stood, but one of them appeared to have a bone pierced through his nose.

The third man, white with dark hair, was dressed in a stunning, brand-new white safari suit, with jodhpur trousers that bulged at the hips and thighs and then disappeared into sleek, black riding boots. A tight-fitting safari jacket covered his chest, and on his head he wore a brand-new, white pith helmet.

He wore glasses, and from what I could make out from across the room, his eyebrows had been painted with something shiny black and thick, making them twice the normal size, and the same black stuff had been used to paint a moustache on the man's face. The man waved a cigar with one hand as he spoke quickly, and in an animated fashion, to Daisy and his uncle.

I inched closer. The man looked up, and then pointed his cigar directly at me. "That's the boy I want," he said. "Money is no object. And objects are no money. But I'd rather have the money, if you're offering. Bring me that boy and we'll talk price later. Did somebody say money? Well, now, I'm all ears. If there's money on the table, bring me two chairs and a bottle of your best wine, waiter. On second thought, make that one chair and more money."

Groups of boys stood off to the side, not daring to get closer.

"The African explorer!"

"Hooray."

"Hooray."

"Hooray."

The two other men, the ones dressed like African natives, walked towards me. When they were five feet away, I recognized them. They were Adolph and Milton Marx. The man in the safari outfit was Julius, of course.

"We've come to rescue you," said Adolph under his breath. He was the one with a prop bone stuck through his nose. "Just play along."

"You look ridiculous."

"Shut up, Josh."

He stood on one side of me, holding my arm, and Milton stood on the other. Without another word, they marched me up to Julius and stopped.

Julius looked me up and down, flicked ash from the cigar to the floor, and said, "Yes, this one will do. He'd look fine in a hunting party. And safarwe haven't been wrong. If you need a minute to figure that one out, I'll give it to you. Put a ribbon around him, will you? He's going to be a Christmas present to my lion. And if you think I'm lion to you, then you've got another fib coming."

He cocked his head in the direction of the door and said, "Now, get him out of here, before I change my mind. Or before he changes his." Adolph and Milton nodded and steered me towards the door.

"Nice and easy," whispered Milton, holding my arm tight. "And here, I think this belongs to you." I felt him slip something into my hand. It was my grouch bag.

We stepped outside, with Julius, Daisy and his uncle a few feet behind us and Julius continuing a non-stop monologue to distract them. There was a car waiting, with another man sitting behind the wheel. He wore thick goggles and a tight flyer's cap pulled low over his forehead, with an aviator's scarf wrapped around his throat. The car was surrounded by boys, several of whom were crying, because they hoped they'd be the one chosen to go back to Africa.

I spotted the boy called Leslie Townes who had been so kind to me, and broke away from the grasp of Adolph and Milton. I reached into the grouch bag, found the twenty-dollar bill, and slipped it to him. "Take this," I said. "This money will buy your way out of here. And Harry Lillis, too."

The boy's eyes grew wide and he clutched the bill, and quickly stuffed it inside his shirt where it couldn't be seen. "Geez," he said. "Thanks a million."

"Your name," I said. "What's your real name? Daisy gave you fake names but what did they call you before you came here?"

He looked around to be sure that Daisy was out of earshot. He bit his lip and thought hard. "I think my real name is Egon," he whispered. "Egon Markowitz."

My mouth dropped open and I gaped at the little boy, speechless. But then Adolph and Milton were back at my side, stuffing me into the car. Julius was backing away from Daisy and his uncle. The uncle was saying, in a loud voice, "Now wait a minute. Just hold your horses. What about the corduroy order?"

"Cordawho? Cordahow?" said Julius. "Say, I'll give the orders around here. I'll take a dozen," he yelled over his shoulder. "No, make that twelve dozen. Or a gross, whichever is cheaper. Gotta dash, the meter is running. Uganda come and visit us sometime. Don't be a stranger. Or at least, any stranger than you already are." Julius jumped onto the running board of the car, grabbed the window to hold on, and yelled, "Punch it!"

The driver sprang to life, jamming the car into gear and stomping on the accelerator pedal. The car jumped forward, swerved to avoid Daisy and his uncle, and shot across the rough ground. Adolph and Milton grabbed Julius and pulled him in through a window. The car sped across the open field, swerved to narrowly avoid crashing into a tree and then just missed creaming one of the security guards who was frantically waving for us to stop. Two other guards were trying to close the gate to seal off our escape, but the driver was able to ram the fence and knock them off their feet.

And then we were in darkness, flying across another field, with the glow of the factory lights receding behind us, making our getaway.

Much later, when I had time to pause and reflect on my rescue from the Oneida Mills, I realized that I was carrying a new memory around inside my head. The memory had the feel and shape of a family story, one of those things that is repeated as family lore many times while you're growing up and has the quality of any bit of family history that has been with you since before you were old enough to know much of anything. It was just in there now, firmly placed in the back of my mind. But, I realized, it had never been in there before. This memory was somehow both old and brand new at the same time.

The memory was a story that, way back in time, my great-grandfather had been given a new start in life. A miracle had happened that changed everything for him and for the Markowitz family's fortunes. A stranger had given him something – a gift, maybe, or money – that totally transformed his life and allowed him to start down a path of great success and fortune.

The great-grandfather, Egon Markowitz, had used the gift to escape horrific poverty and lead a long and happy life filled with laughter and benevolence. He established a tradition of giving back that carried over with every future Markowitz generation.

Repeated a hundred years later, its details blurred, the story now resembled a myth or a fable more than an actual event. The family fable was that you never know where good might come from in your life, and you should always remain cheerful and open to the possibility that something wonderful could happen every single day of your life.

In 1908, I, Josh Markowitz, the class clown, was creating family history. Kind of cool.

CHAPTER TWENTY-TWO: AUTOPIA

We drove for an hour without stopping, and then the driver pulled over at a clearing and got out. The air was crisp and clear and a million stars were in the night sky. He took off the scarf and goggles and aviator hat. It was Leonard, of course, but before I could move in for the swift kick that I had planned back in the paddy wagon, he held up a hand.

"Josh, I can explain," said Lenny Marx. "Hear me out. We sent you up the river for your own good."

I stomped my feet, turned two circles in sheer anger, picked up a rock and chucked it as far as I could into the field, and let out a scream of frustration that made birds flush and fly away from the trees. "I got to clean out buckets of poop and carry more buckets of toxic waste *for my own good*?"

"In a manner of speaking," said Lenny. "Maybe not pleasant, but it was better than being dead or in jail."

"Which is what we tell ourselves every time we go on the road and end up in a place like Scranton," said Julius.

Leonard stepped forward and patted me on the cheek. "I'm really sorry, Josh. We had no choice. The streets were crawling with coppers looking for you, and there is no telling what they would have done if they caught you. At least this way we knew where you were being taken and we could rescue you. Getting you off the street took the heat away."

Adolph nodded. "Took us longer than we expected to rustle up the car and the costumes. And we got a little lost. Everything looks the same once you're out of the city. Sorry about that, Josh."

Julius laughed. "The African explorer. Well that was certainly the most ridiculous thing we've ever done. I can't believe that we got away with that. You know," he said, turning to Leonard, "we were really funny. That's the kind of comedy that I can see us doing. I can't imagine that anybody would ever want to pay to see us do things like that. But it was sure fun."

Leonard nodded and slapped him on the back. "I think so, too."

I still had my hands balled up into fists. "Can't blame you for being mad," Leonard said. "How about we make it up to you? You can drive the car."

"You're kidding," I said. "I'm only twelve."

"Nah, go ahead. We just learned how to drive yesterday. There's really nothing to it."

So I got to drive, all night long through the deserted part of upstate New York. It was pretty fun – kind of like a videogame mixed with Autopia at Disneyland. But outside the town of Saugerties, the car started to make coughing sounds, and then it died.

"Did you bring more gas?" Adolph asked Leonard.

"I thought you did."

"Well don't look at me," said Julius. "I'm a city boy. Where am I supposed to get gas? At Kornblatt's deli? Wait a minute, don't answer that."

"Let's go find some."

Milton was asleep in the car, so the four of us walked down the road until we came upon a farm. Leonard walked to the door of the house and started pounding on it.

"Are you kidding me?" I said. "In my day, you get shot when you pound on someone's door at three in the morning."

"You know, you paint a real rosy picture of the future," said Julius. "I think I'm gonna stay right here in the past, where it's safe. Of course we're going to ask the farmer. How else are we going to get gas at this hour?"

A woman in a long bathrobe opened the door a moment later, and after a brief wait, the farmer stumbled out, still hitching up his overalls. He led us to the barn, where he hand-pumped gasoline from a rusty old tank into four large coffee cans. He refused to take money, and before we left, his wife brought us four sandwiches wrapped in waxed paper. The brothers and I thanked them, and were on our way.

Leonard got behind the wheel and I sat next to him. Julius and Adolph climbed into the back seat next to Milton, ate their sandwiches, ate his sandwich, too, and were asleep in minutes.

"Josh, I've gotta tell it to you straight. You scare me." It was the middle of the night, Leonard was driving, and I've never seen as many stars in my life in the night sky as when I stuck my head out the window. "I don't know what we're gonna do with you."

"How do you mean, Lenny?" I asked.

"Look," he said, turning to me as he kept one hand on the wheel and steered the car. "I asked everybody I know about you. EVERYBODY. And I know a lotta people. And not one of them knew a thing about you. Had never heard of you even. A kid who tells a story that he has come all the way from Oregon. Well, it's 1908, Josh, and kids your age don't just show up in New York City from places like that. They're still fighting Indians and stuff out west."

I was tired. I had no fight left in me. Nothing was clear to me anymore after getting a glimpse of how some kids' lives went at the textile factory. Either doomed to die there or to never leave, as if they didn't have a single choice or opportunity in their whole lives. For once in my life I didn't have a funny way to look at it, or a joke to put it into perspective.

"I'm not a liar. I never have been. Whether you believe me or not, it's true," I said quietly.

"Well, maybe so," he said. "Hey, stranger things have happened, I guess. Look, Josh." He suddenly stopped the car and turned to face me fully. His eyes were blazing. "I LOVE the idea of the Marx Brothers being funny. I would do ANYTHING to make that true. But it would take something that I don't think we have. You get me? Telling jokes and acting silly, like we were back at the factory? I don't see us being able to make that change on stage and have any chance at all for a happy life for me and my brothers. Mostly because our mother would kill us if we tried to change the act behind her back."

He turned back to the wheel and continued to drive. There was a long silence. And then something came to me. Maybe something that I had known all along but just hadn't realized, like a lingering thing in the back of your mind that takes its time to come forward. Or maybe more like something that has been in front of you for your whole life but it was in such plain sight that you ignored it long enough that you no longer even saw it. Like how you love your mom and dad. Or how you've kept a favorite stuffed animal around even though you're way past the age when you really wanted or needed it (okay, total disclosure: It's a stuffed carrot, for me. Yes, I keep a big orange and green carrot on my bed. I've had it since I was three. I love my carrot and it loves me.)

"It takes guts," I finally said. "If you want to be funny, you have to have guts. And you have to believe in yourself. You put your soul out there on the line every time you try to be funny. Kids make fun of you, teachers send you downstairs for punishment, the assistant principal gives you detention, the stupid kids who don't get the jokes hate you and threaten to beat you up. One mean person says, 'Oh Josh isn't funny,' and it breaks your heart. But you keep doing it because it's something deep inside you.

"Maybe you're right, Lenny, and you and your brothers just don't have what it takes to be comedians."

His mouth tightened into an angry line. "You're saying that the Marx Brothers don't have any guts?"

I shrugged. "I don't know if you do or you don't, but what I'm hearing is that you don't have the nerve to even try. I'm saying that you already know that you're funny. I came all the way here from the future to tell you that you're funny and will have a great future. All you need to do is just trust your instincts. And you won't even do that because you're afraid of your mother.

"And you're afraid of failure. You just must not have that special thing that it takes to succeed. I'm obviously wasting my time here."

I looked out the window and my heart sank lower than it ever has in my life. "So much time," I said softly. "All the time in the world."

"You're just a kid who likes to tell stories," snarled Leonard. "And I'll tell you what, Josh. Once we get back to New York City, we're gonna part ways. You can find another family to play make-believe with. The Marx family will do just fine without you."

I didn't even care. I nodded and said, "Fine. You want proof, but there is no proof. You either believe in yourself and your brothers or you don't. You accept the story I'm telling you as truth or you don't. Nobody knows if the joke is funny before they tell it; they have to wait for the laugh. So you take a chance and tell the joke.

"So go ahead and don't believe that I'm telling you the truth. I don't care. But how are you going to spend your life, Lenny? What are you going to do with that talent you've been given that makes people like you and makes people laugh?"

He drove on in silence, and then finally said. "I'll think of something."

Quietly, from the back seat, Julius said, "So will I."

And then a second later, Adolph concurred. Not by speaking, but by HONKing.

CHAPTER TWENTY-THREE: A CLOWN NAMED SLIVERS

We drove on in silence. There was really nothing left to say. When we got back to New York I was going to try to figure out how to get back to my own time. I had no idea how I was going to do that. And the Marx Brothers were going to go on stage on Coney Island as the Four Nightingales, sing a few songs, and go on with their lives. I couldn't wait to get on Google when (and if) I got home and find out what became of them. Maybe that newspaper article that Slivers showed me about them going to jail after their singing act broke up was the real truth, and all of the other stuff – the movies, the TV shows, the books, the stories about the hilarious Marx Brothers – would all vanish from the historical record as if it were made of dust. History would be erased and rewritten as easily as a hard drive on a computer crashing, and the only people of my time who would remember the Marx Brothers as comedians would be me and a weird old clown named Slivers.

What else would be erased with them? Without the Marx Brothers, maybe there is no Saturday Night

Live show, or any other humor that comes from being clever and irreverent. Without SNL, maybe there is no Jimmy Fallon or Jimmy Kimmel, and the late-night shows are just boring old men interviewing scientists and politicians. No Jim Carrey acting silly. No Ben Stiller joking and being witty. No Will Farrell making outlandish vids. No South Park or 30 Rock or Malcom in the Middle. Nothing.

There would be a lot of unraveling. The world wouldn't be as funny. But I had tried, and done the best I could. I will always be able to say that I tried my best.

As dawn broke, we all realized that we were starving. Leonard spotted a boarding house and drove the car across a field to get to it. A kindly woman greeted us at the door, pointed to a pump and trough in the yard where we could wash our hands and faces, and in no time at all the five of us were sitting around a big dining room table that was loaded with stacks of ham and eggs, thick slices of homemade bread and pancakes with butter and syrup, all washed down with pottery pitchers full of milk and coffee and cream. I have never been so hungry in my life, and food never looked more delicious than it did that morning. It was the first time I ever tried coffee, too, and I found it to be hot and bitter and delicious. It was also the first decent meal I had had in four days, and I put the food away like I was the starting offensive line for the Green Bay Packers.

"The kid from Oregon can sure sock away the chow," said Julius as I reached for my fourth slice of ham.

"I'll say," his brothers all chimed in.

"The future is a dark and hungry place," said Adolph. He reached over and mussed my hair. I sure liked Adolph. Of all of the Marx Brothers, I think that he needed comedy the most. He had too gentle a spirit to do the hustling that Leonard and Julius would be able to manage in their lives to get by. He would get chewed up in the world of business and having to keep jobs to make a living.

When we were nearly finished, Leonard reached into his pocket. "Hey Josh, I think this is yours," he said. "I found it near your bed in Mama's apartment."

He handed over a small coin, which I realized at once was the token that Slivers had given me that would operate The Great Wandini. I had totally forgotten about it. Not that it mattered much. I had no idea where to find The Great Wandini, and New York City was a rather large place to find it.

"Looks like a streetcar token," said Julius. "Maybe you need that to ride the streetcar back to the future." He was teasing. They still didn't believe me.

"Maybe I do," I said. "Slivers gave this to me just before I left my time. He warned me not to lose it. I'm glad you found it. Thanks."

The room went dead quiet. Everybody stopped eating except me. I stuffed another half a pancake

into my mouth and then looked up to see the four
Marx Brothers staring at me. Their faces had drained
of color and their mouths hung open. Like they'd just
seen a ghost.

"What?" I said.

"Did you say Slivers?" asked Leonard.

"Slivers the Clown?" Julius added. His voice
was suddenly hoarse.

"Yeah. What about him?" I said.

Adolph put his hand on my arm. "Are you
telling us that you have met a clown named Slivers?"

"He's the one who sent me here. Didn't I ever
tell you guys that?"

"NO!" the four Marx Brothers nearly shouted
in unison.

"And maybe you could have not taken six days
to bring it up?" said Leonard.

Julius motioned to the woman to bring more
coffee. "Well, this changes everything, doesn't it?" he
said. "You'd better tell us what you know about
Slivers the Clown, Josh. And take your time. We've
waited our whole lives to hear this."

I finished the pancake. "You know about him?"

"He's a legend," said Leonard quietly.
"Nobody compares to Slivers the Clown. His real
name is Frank Oakley. He's amazing."

Adolph nodded. "I went to see Oakley perform at the Hippodrome last year. He was unbelievable. He held an audience of 8,000 people in the palm of his hand. They were crying, they laughed so hard. And there he was, alone onstage, in full clown makeup and costume and never said a word. It was genius. Sheer genius."

"Well, maybe he was funny once," I said, "but when I met him last week he was kind of a creepy old man."

Speaking of creepy, the Marx Brothers once again were pale as ghosts and staring at me.

"Go on," Julius croaked.

So I told them the whole story. How I had never heard of a clown in our town, but all of a sudden on the day that I got in trouble at school for being the Class Clown, here comes this note to visit Slivers the Clown in his creepy, old, abandoned warehouse on the wrong side of McMinnville. I tried to describe the Groucho Glasses that he sent with the note, and couldn't, so I drew a picture of them on a piece of paper.

Leonard shot Julius a questioning look and bit his lip. "Why didn't I think of that?" muttered Julius. "Go on, Josh, don't stop."

So I described going into the shop, and the Great Wandini, and how Slivers said he was something like 150 years old. And how the next thing I knew I was almost cut in half by a streetcar, and Julius saved me.

"That's it," I said. "That's my story, and I'm sticking to it. Whether you geniuses believe me or not."

Julius let out a long breath. "You don't seem to remember this, Josh, but you didn't just pop up on the street next to that streetcar. I watched you emerge from a cellar door and kind of stagger onto the street, and that's when I came and gave you a little push. I mean, it was you or the streetcar, and I didn't like those odds very well."

"You're right," I said. "I don't remember anything about a cellar. I must have still been in a daze from the time travel."

Leonard frowned. "Yeah," he said quietly, "from the time travel. Because we all believe in time travel."

I got up from the table. I was stuffed from all the food, but I also realized that I had to get going if I was going to have any chance of getting home before the seven-day deadline passed. "Sorry, guys, I'd love to stay and chat with you Marx Brothers, whoever you might end up being in history. But I've really got to get back to New York City and try to get home. Could we all please get in the car again?"

Julius and Leonard both put their hands on my arms, pulling me back down in my chair.

"Hang on a second, Josh," said Julius. "We have something now that we need to tell you."

Leonard nodded. "You really did see a ghost named Slivers, Josh. And you really did travel back through time to find us."

Adolph nodded. "And the amazing thing is that you've lived to tell about it. And speaking for my brothers, I have one important thing to tell you."

He leaned in closer and looked into my eyes. "We totally believe you now, Josh. And we want to thank you."

Leonard and Julius and Milton all nodded in agreement. "Yes we do," Julius finally said with a catch in his throat. "I've never believed in miracles before."

"But this is a miracle," said Leonard. "A miracle for the Marx Brothers.

"And for you. Josh from Oregon. The Class Clown who saved comedy."

Then the Marx Brothers did something silly: They jumped off of their chairs and got down on their knees and began to bow and prostrate themselves on the floor, moaning, "Oh save us, oh Josh from Oregon. Save us! Deliver us to the comic land! We're not worthy, we're not worthy!"

"Oh, cut it out," I said. I was grinning. "What a bunch of idiots."

CHAPTER TWENTY-FOUR: BE VERY FUNNY

We paid and thanked the woman for the incredible breakfast, which cost a grand total of 55 cents, and went back to the car. "Milton, you drive," commanded Leonard as we all piled into the car. "We've got to get Josh ready for the show, and tell him something important."

As the youngest Marx brother took the wheel and pointed the car towards New York City, the other brothers crowded around me in the back seat.

"Okay, here's the deal, Josh," said Adolph. "This is why we believe you. Frank Oakley, who is Slivers the Clown in our time, has always been rumored to have some kind of supernatural powers."

"It's just that he's so good," added Leonard quickly. "And he came out of nowhere. He arrives on the scene from the middle of nothing, like the plains of Kansas or Nebraska, and suddenly, within a year he's headlining the Hippodrome and people are literally screaming with laughter at his shows. Nobody had ever seen anything like it. It's like he is not of this Earth."

"Or this time," continued Julius. "We thought at first it was a bunch of malarkey, but as we have become more involved in show business, we have heard many times about a legend. A spirit that people have seen and touched and felt. But until ten minutes and fourteen pancakes ago, we thought it was all a bunch of nonsense."

I was trying to keep up with this three-headed Marx explanation. They were all talking so fast and cutting in on each other that it was hard to follow. "What legend? What spirit?" I asked. "What are you talking about?"

"There is a legend in show business circles," said Julius, "that there is some kind of ghost or spirit that has appeared through history that inspires performers."

"Especially comedians," said Adolph.

Leonard nodded. "Almost exclusively comedians. We have heard it described in many ways. A beautiful woman comes along and inspires or encourages someone. Or a wizard..."

"...or a genie," said Adolph.

"Or a dog, or a cat, or a vase that falls on their head," added Julius. "We've heard this darned story told every which way. But you're the first person to explain it as a clown. And that makes a lot of sense."

"And it makes sense that Frank Oakley took on the name and character of a spirit that calls itself Slivers the Clown and had this sudden, amazing success," said Leonard. "There have been rumors for years that there was something a little weird and unusual about the guy. I've tried to get close to him for years and never have been able to. It's like he vanishes into thin air after his shows. Nobody ever sees him out and about in the city. But people who have performed on the same bill with him have told me over and over that he had some kind of weird connection to something that they didn't understand."

"Something that gave him the strength to be a great comic," said Adolph. "And believe me, I don't use this word often, but he was truly great."

Julius clapped me on the back. "To have the guts, as you put it. You're right. It takes a lot of guts to be a comedian."

"And something else," said Adolph. "It takes the confidence to know that you're doing the right thing and aren't just going off half-baked trying to act like you're funny. When I saw Slivers Oakley perform at the Hippodrome, you could tell that he was sure, he was absolutely certain, of his act and his talent and his place in history. It was like he was gathering some energy from far, far away and using it in his act."

Leonard nodded. "It was the spirit. It was the spirit of that old man who visited you that got into Frank Oakley. He took the name Slivers the Clown and off he went. Within a year he was playing packed houses."

I shook my head. I was amazed by what they were saying. "And for some reason that spirit chose me to visit you and tell you to turn to comedy?"

Julius pursed his lips and nodded. "For some reason, it did. And now I have only one question for my brothers."

"Yeah?" asked the other three, including Milton in the front seat.

"What are we going to tell our mother?"

They laughed. "Leave it to me," said Leonard. "I'll take care of Minnie."

Adolph elbowed me in the ribs. "Josh, what are our stage names again?"

"You seriously want to know?"

He nodded. So did Leonard and Julius. "Okay, but I'm warning you that once you know them you'll never go back to your given names. You will use these names exclusively for the rest of your lives, and even refer to each other by these names. I don't know why. You just do."

"Tell us."

"Okay. Julius, you're Groucho. For a couple of obvious reasons, but also for the not so obvious reason that you always wear a grouch bag with your money safely stored in it."

He grinned. "That works. Kind of suits my mood most of the time, too."

"Sure does," said Adolph. "Truer words have never been spoken."

"And Adolph, naturally, you're Harpo."

He nodded and smiled. "I like that just fine. It makes me want to practice and get better at my instrument."

"What about me?" asked Milton from the front seat.

"Gummo," I said. "You will like shoes with rubber soles, like a detective wears. So you're Gummo."

He frowned. "What a stupid name."

"Sorry," I said, "I didn't make these up. I'm just telling you. Your brother Herbert has a funny name, too. Zeppo, from the zeppelins."

"Ha, I like that. Zeppo. And me?" asked Leonard. "What was it you called me? Sicko, Birdie, Dames-O?"

I shook my head. "You're close. You're Chico. Pronounced Chick-O. You know why?"

He smiled, happy, and rubbed his hands together with glee. "I sure do. This is gonna be great. I'm gonna meet so many girls. Who would you rather date, a Leonard or a Chico?" He held out his fist and his brothers, including Milton from the front seat, all topped it with their hands.

"Ladies and gentlemen," he announced, "I give you the new Marx Brothers."

Harpo laughed. "And our fearless leader, Josh Markowitz, the Class Clown."

Groucho agreed. "Heretofore known to one and all as . . . wait for it . . . Marko!"

I put my fist on top of theirs and we all laughed.

A half-hour later we entered the city. "Where are you going to drop me off?" I asked.

"Drop you off?" said Groucho. "Are you nuts?"

Harpo grinned. "You're coming with us, Josh. We're not going to let you out of our sight."

Chico turned to me. "Are you ready for show business, Josh? Today's going to be your big debut. You're the fifth nightingale."

"And the last one, too," I said. "I think the question is, is show business ready for me?"

He laughed. "You're going to do great. Just follow your instincts. You've got good instincts, kid."

I nodded. "So is today the day that the Marx Brothers become a comedy act?"

"You bet your life it is," Groucho said softly.

Chico nodded and looked serious. "If it doesn't work, you know, they'll never allow us on a stage again. Vaudeville producers don't take kindly to a singing act that don't sing. Our performing careers will be over, just like that."

Harpo just laughed. "But what could go wrong? Listen, Josh, just do us all a favor. If you're going to be funny…

"…be *very* funny." He looked over at me and slapped me on the knee.

"The Marx Brothers will do the rest."

Groucho stared out the window for a minute, and then added, "How we're going to do it is anybody's guess."

CHAPTER TWENTY-FIVE: FROM THE DIARY OF OMAR SPARROW

There were only two tokens left. Two! When we started this there were, like, two dozen. But then all of the kids got wind of The Great Wandini, and the students of Patton Middle School were off to the races. Spring break had never been, and I'm willing to bet will never again be like this.

Talk about living history. It got out that Stevie San Pedro and Elizabeth Walcot Woolcott had gone off to England in the 18somethings to watch a play. A play! And when they get back Stevie is wearing a monocle all the time and carrying a cane, and he wears this tuxedo everywhere he goes, even to baseball practice, and starts referring to everyone and his dog as "Old Chap." I say, Old Chap, would you mind tossing me the ball so I can complete the double play? Awfully good of you, old chap. Cripes.

Jackson goes back to the 1980s to watch his namesake Michael Jackson perform Thriller. Lisa and Stan want to go to a Spice Girls concert. Humberto has always wanted to be a Ninja so he heads for Japan in the Shogun period and comes back with a wicked cool set of hand-stitched body armor and a big sword. Tiny little Kyrie

Vigens, all 47 pounds of her, goes way way back and teaches the primitive people how to make fire. And the wheel. She thought it would be cool to teach Neanderthal man how to stay warm and roll things.

So she did. Well, somebody had to do it. They probably would have gotten around to it eventually, but she jumpstarted civilization by a couple of hundred years.

Two tokens. It's late at night and I'm worried about my friend, Josh. There has been no more word from him, and I do a deep search of the old newspapers every day at the library, hoping for another mention of him. Nothing. I know that he got his name in the paper on purpose so we could find him, and now it scares me that he has vanished again into time. I go back to the warehouse and look at the typeset page, and nothing changes. I try leaving a couple of messages for Slivers the Clown. Still nothing; no answer. I'm concerned that Josh is stuck in the past with no way back. I'm also concerned that if any more tokens are found for The Great Wandini, we'll be holding our 7th-grade spring picnic in Hawaii before it was discovered by Captain James Cook.

I'm not altogether crazy about this concept of time travel. As usual, I don't have a dime to my name, and I typically think it would be a good idea to time-travel with a few bucks in your pocket. If you want to buy a hot dog or something in the past. I'm also not really positive that it works, and that the kids aren't all making up their amazing trips to the past. I mean, Tallulah and Sierra O'Donnell said they went to the 1936 Olympics in Germany and showed up at Serendipity wearing "We

Jesse Owens" t-shirts, and according to my library research, nobody was hearting much of anything in Germany in 1936.

Curiously, diary, the only person who stayed put and didn't time travel was Amy Connors, who says she likes it right here in Yamhill County just fine, and why would she want to go anyplace else, or any other time, if it meant leaving her mom and dad and cat behind. I kind of like that about her. My family has moved about eighteen times, and the idea of staying in one place holds a kind of wistful appeal for me.

"I'm good," she said when I asked if she wanted to come with me to find Josh, and then she made me a butter and marshmallow fluff sandwich. "Good luck, Omar," she said. "Tell Josh I said hi if you find him. I'm sure Lizzie would say the same."

But best friends do as best friends will, and Josh needs me. I put one of the last two remaining tokens in my pocket, because I'd like to come back one day. I grasp the Great Wandini's smooth, wooden hand. I drop the token into the slot and all kinds of lights and noise start whizzing around me like I'm standing on the infield of the Daytona 500 car race. I say, "Coney Island, April 27th, 1908."

I shut my eyes.

I don't know how I get myself into these things. Honest, I don't.

Sparrow out.

CHAPTER TWENTY-SIX: EXCUSE US

Henderson's Beer Garden on Coney Island was an indoor/outdoor theater that started with a big open tent covering a bare floor that was ankle-deep in sawdust. The air smelled of the beer that was poured from kegs into buckets by enormous, burly men in sleeveless t-shirts who, had they lived in my time, looked like they could be the starting defensive line of the New York Giants. From the buckets, the beer was then poured into big, glass steins for people to buy for a nickel, which they did often and with great enthusiasm. Even though it was a warm, weekend day the men in the audience were dressed in suits, with bow ties and top hats, and the women wore long, flowing dresses and boots that laced up past their ankles.

"These people need to invent casual Friday and cargo shorts," I muttered to myself after we had been there an hour, putting on our costumes for the show. Everyone looked totally hot and uncomfortable.

Other vendors sold hot dogs and pretzels and peanuts. Lingering over the whole scene was the crisp, salty smell of the Atlantic Ocean, just behind the building. It was hot and humid, and the rough fabric of the white, Four Nightingales costume made me sweat and itch.

The sawdust area under the tent gave way to a rickety building, inside of which were rows of auditorium seats and benches facing a big stage with a purple, velvet curtain. More beer was served in there, and people could stagger in with their glasses from the tent, get refills and slug it down as they watched the show. It seemed to be a dead toss-up on whether they came for the beer or the entertainment, but the beer definitely appeared to be pulling ahead. A hand-painted sign at the door called out, "Vaudeville Show Today! Amazing Feats of Skill and Daring! The Most Talented Singers! The Funniest Comics and Spell-Binding MagiciansI Miss Penelope and Her Midget Dachsunds! Beer for a Nickel!"

"Yeah, amazing feats of daring," I said. "They don't know the half of it. I dare them to hear me sing."

"Ah, you'll do fine," said Chico. "Just pretend the audience is naked. Or pretend that you're naked. Just do us both a favor and don't pretend that I'm naked. If you pretend I'm naked, I'm gonna have to bust you one in the chops."

"Say, look at you," Groucho said, admiring my costume. "Why you look just like a regular nightingale."

"Yeah, Florence Nightingale," I said.

"Ha, good one, Josh, but maybe you should leave the jokes to the professional comedians," he said.

Minnie arrived wearing a fancy hat and coat that went with her worried frown. She ordered everyone to get ready, act professional, don't bring shame to the family. "This is how we pay our rent," she reminded her sons. "This is our business and our lives." The ultimate stage mother was in her element.

She took one look at me in the costume and makeup, sighed, and said, "As for you, keep your mouth shut. Just pretend that you're singing."

"I'll pretend I don't hear him pretending to sing," offered Groucho.

"And I'll pretend I didn't hear you say that," said Chico. "In fact, I'll pretend I wasn't even here if that would make you happy."

Minnie just threw her hands up and bustled off to talk to the manager about our spot in the lineup.

Vaudeville was a form of entertainment for the masses where all kinds of acts were brought together at a theater like Henderson's to perform, one after the other, for crowds who wanted to get away from their lives and work and cramped apartments for a few hours. The acts could be anything: Guys with trained dogs that jumped through hoops, operatic tenors who belted out classical songs, comedians, impressionists, ventriloquists, actors who recited dramatic scenes from Shakespeare, circus performers doing stunts, and cowboys riding their horses on stage and reenacting mock battles with Indians who were actually a bunch of guys named Ed from Staten Island in fake, feathered headdresses.

The Four Nightingales were scheduled to go on three times, right after an act where a guy balanced spinning dishes on poles while his wife/assistant danced around in a tutu. Minnie rehearsed our entrance. We would march single-file behind Groucho onto the stage to the tune of "Swanee River," waving our hats and smiling like little angels.

"I have such a bad feeling about this," she said as we waited in the wings to go on. "Really, I don't know how you boys talk me into these things."

Finally, it was our turn. The broken plates were swept aside, the lady in the tutu gave one last bow to a smattering of applause, the master of ceremonies said a few choice words, and then Chico, who had been drafted at the last minute to play the piano, was walking onto the stage with his music, an angelic smile plastered onto his face. He seated himself at the piano and began to play.

"Well, here goes nothing," said Groucho.

My thoughts exactly. I had butterflies the size of cinderblocks in my stomach. And for all of my talk and good intentions about arriving at the moment where I could help the Marx Brothers become comedians, and change their lives, and put the history of comedy on the course that I would know and love, I could not for the life of me think of a single funny thing to do or say. My mouth felt like the Sahara Desert and my knees had a funny way of shaking inside my pants.

At the last minute before we went on, I had a bright idea and ran back to our dressing room. I knew that Harpo would have left his honking cab horn in there with his street clothes, and I grabbed it, ran back to the stage and shoved it into his pants.

"I've got a feeling you're going to need this," I said.

"Thanks, Josh," he said. From that day forward, Harpo would always perform in pantomime, a mute who got some of the biggest laughs in the history of the theater.

Walking onto the stage was terrifying, and I had a sudden spell of dizziness and panic that nearly made me faint. I didn't even mean to do anything funny at first, but when we marched on stage I got out of step behind Harpo and in front of Gummo, had to stop twice and rearrange my steps and kind of hopped around like my socks where on fire, which made the audience laugh. The sound came up as a gentle swell to my left, a rumbling, tangible thing, and when I stopped and turned to look at them, the expression on my face was so surprised and pleased that it got another laugh.

"Not yet," Groucho hissed in my ear as he got me back into line. "Just wait a minute with the hijinks."

I couldn't bear to tell him that I had no hijinks up my sleeve, nor could I think of a single funny thing to do or say. He finished *Swanee River*, broke into *My Old Kentucky Home*, and then we all did *Yankee Doodle*, with me mouthing the words because I didn't have a clue what they were. There was mild applause after each number, but even I could tell that the audience was getting restless and we were losing them.

And then it was time for *Oranges and Lemons*, an old English rhyme about the sounds that church bells make that was set to music and was one of the most popular songs of the early-1900s. Everybody in the room knew that song . . . except me. The boys had told me in the car that when it was my turn, I was supposed to step forward, turn and face the audience, and sing, "You owe me five farthings, say the bells of St. Martin's."

But I had completely forgotten what they said. Which was good, because nobody told me what a farthing was.

The song began, and Groucho sang, "Oranges and lemons, say the bells of St. Clements." He stepped back into line and looked at me.

Harpo looked at me.

Gummo looked at me.

In the wings, Minnie looked at me and mouthed the words, "Go! Your turn!" At the piano, Chico played my cue again…and then again.

Groucho arched what would become his famous eyebrows at me. His face, locked in the smile that he was supposed to wear on stage, looked pained and terrified. He knew stage fright when he saw it; it was written all over my face. He slipped his hand onto my back and practically pushed me forward, towards the audience.

I felt like I was naked and the whole world was staring at me. I couldn't remember my line. Couldn't even remember where I was, or why I was there. All I could see was a sea of faces sitting in front of me, and they were getting restless. I could practically feel the rotten tomatoes and eggs that they had hidden away in their pockets, the better to chuck at comedians who aren't funny and singers who can't remember their cues.

I looked right, and then left. And then a song popped into my head, and it was literally the only song I could remember.

But it wasn't Oranges and Lemons. The song that represented the sum total of my musical knowledge started this way.

"Are you ready, kids?" I shouted to the audience. "I said, are you ready?"

And then as if my mouth was being controlled by some demon from the future, I belted out, "Who lives in a pineapple under the sea? Spongebob squarepants.

"Absorbent and yellow and porous is he. Spongebob squarepants. If nautical nonsense be something you wish, then drop on the deck and flop like a fish."

The only song in the vast universe of music that I could remember was the theme song from Spongebob Squarepants. A show that wouldn't even get its start for about a hundred years. On a device known as television that was still fifty years away from being invented.

Oops.

The place went dead quiet. The sound of two hundred fifty people sucking in their breath and holding it all at once is an interesting thing, like a gale wind blowing backwards. I realized, too late, what I had just said to an entire vaudeville audience, and my hand flew up to cover my mouth.

The Marx Brothers stood dead still on stage, still wearing their stage smiles. And then a single, piercing sound rang out behind me.

HOOOONNNNKKK!

Harpo looked around innocently, as if he hadn't heard or done anything. And then he did it again, squeezing the horn that was hidden inside his costume.

HOOOONNNNKKK!

And that's when I came to my senses. I took one step closer to the audience. I shook my head and held up one hand in a gesture of apology.

And then I shouted, "Well, excuuuussssseeeee me!"

The whole place went nuts. People roared with laughter. The sound was like thunder that literally shook us on the stage. I looked to my left, and Minnie had fainted dead away in the wings. Chico, at the piano, was holding his hand over his eyes trying to mask his own laughter, which made his shoulders shake.

Groucho looked at Harpo and nodded, and then Harpo looked at Chico. The comic instincts of the Marx Brothers took over from there, kicking it into high gear. Harpo ran over to Minnie, dragged her by the legs onto the stage and began to fan her with his shirt, like it was all part of the act. Chico jumped up from the piano, ran over to them and began fanning Harpo with HIS shirt, and then the brothers fanned each other. The audience roared its approval.

Groucho stepped to center stage where I was standing and put his arm around me. I wasn't sure if he was going to slug me or kick me off the stage. Instead, he turned to the audience and announced in a loud voice, "Folks, this young nightingale might look like an idiot. And he certainly does sound like an idiot. But I assure you, he really is an idiot."

They went nuts over that, too, and Groucho kept going. He walked over to Minnie, who was just sitting up, and said, "Excuse me, Madam, would you like some lemon sauce with your flounder?"

"Aw, leave her alone," yelled Chico, "she's not herring you too good."

The brothers began to dash around the stage, chasing each other, chasing the showgirls from off-stage ONTO the stage and generally cutting loose. Harpo honked his horn and Chico tackled him. The audience howled.

In the midst of the mayhem, someone approached me from behind and grabbed me by the arm. I looked over to see that it was a policeman, and for one frantic second I thought it was Officer Mulcahy, come to take me back to the textile mills.

But then I realized right away that it wasn't Mulcahy. The policeman who was now on stage with me was much shorter. Funny looking. In makeup. He was a young man with old eyes that were instantly familiar to me.

This officer was actually a clown in the costume of a police officer, but with three brightly colored circles down the front of the blue cop uniform. His face was painted white, with blue diamonds at the eyes and big red rectangles on the nose and chin, with a huge, lurid red mouth.

The audience roared with approval and recognition. "Slivers!" they yelled.

Because in his day, Frank "Slivers" Oakley was the most famous clown in the world, the Michael Jordan of circus performers. Everyone knew him. For the audience at Henderson's, it was like if you were at a Taylor Swift concert and Justin Bieber showed up to sing a couple of duets. Slivers grinned, turned and bowed to them and they cheered again.

"You're doing great, kid," he whispered to me, just as Harpo pulled Slivers away and began a hysterical stage fight with the cop, completely in slow-motion pantomime. Chico rushed on-stage and grabbed Harpo's leg, and then everyone was suddenly down on the floor of the stage in a crazy dogpile.

Slivers emerged from the pile to a huge cheer from the audience, pulled out a pair of prop handcuffs and slapped them on me. "Time to go home, kid. Your friend found me in time," he whispered as he marched me off the stage. "Lucky he did, too, because I had completely forgotten."

I played it just right and gave the audience a big wave as I was leaving, and they stood up and cheered the boy who sang about sea sponges.

"Friend? What friend?" I said, but Slivers didn't answer.

My performance with the Marx Brothers earned me my first and only standing ovation. Everyone present agreed that I had a bright future in comedy . . . if I could ever escape from the past, that is.

As Slivers and I left the building we heard the Marx Brothers receive their own standing ovation, their first ever for being funny and telling jokes on the stage. There would be many, many more in the ensuing years and decades as they honed their stage act, played it in theaters all over the country, including on Broadway, and then when the time was right, took their comedy straight to movie screens.

That history that had begun to dry up and turn to dust? It was all rearranging itself and going back to normal as Slivers the Clown and I beat it out of Henderson's.

CHAPTER TWENTY-SEVEN: TEARS OF A CLOWN

A voice behind us called out, "I didn't do it."

To which I immediately replied, "That's what she said." And I've never in my life been happier to see anyone. Omar walked up to me and gave me a big hug, and then we jumped up and down for a while like we had just scored the winning touchdown of the McMinnville Grizzlies homecoming game.

"How did you know…?"

"Oh, everybody knows, Josh. Kids have been going back in time this week like it was a trip to Lincoln City."

I just shook my head at that. I wished we could talk more, but I was still handcuffed to a clown named Slivers and he was dragging me down the Coney Island boardwalk. "Follow us!" I yelled to Omar.

We walked farther down the boardwalk, but then Slivers sank onto a bench. He reached into his shoe and produced a key that unlocked the handcuffs. He then put the key into his mouth, swallowed it, and then put his head in his hands. He looked miserable and as deflated as a birthday balloon that has lost almost all of its helium.

"I'm just really not very good at this business of life," he moaned. He pointed in the direction of Henderson's Music Hall. "That, I'm good at. I can still kill 'em at joints like that. They need ambulances, the people laugh so hard. But this…I just ain't no good at this." He dropped his head into his hands and his shoulders began to shake.

I looked at Omar, he looked at me. We both shrugged and reached a silent agreement: Is there anything more pathetic than a wretched clown? I sat next to Slivers and awkwardly patted him on the back. "It's okay," I said. "You were great. The audience loved you."

"You made their whole day," said Omar. "And you gave the Marx Brothers the start that they needed."

Slivers looked at me and his eyes were wet. "You don't know what it's like, kid. You don't know. I hope for your sake that you're never funny. Because they just won't leave you alone, ever. You make them laugh once, they want to laugh twice. You make them laugh again and they just keep coming at you, wanting more. More, more, more."

He blubbered again, and then began to pull a handkerchief out of his sleeve. He pulled and pulled until the handkerchief was eight feet long...because he was a clown. He blew his nose in a big, exaggerated motion and then stuffed the entire handkerchief back into the front of his pants.

I waited, and waited, and waited for this bit of comedy to be finished. "Okay, I understand. Now, can you take us home?"

"Home where?" he said.

"You know, back to Oregon. Back to our own time."

"Your own time?" Slivers thought about it hard, trying to concentrate and remember. He raised a finger into the air and grinned as if he were having a sudden inspiration, and then dropped the hand and his lips drooped and he dropped his head and was sad again. Then he raised his finger again and the big, stupid clown grin returned. He put the finger to his head as if he were thinking and then triumphantly shook it.

Then he shook his head again, the grin faded into a frown, and he slumped forward, his shoulders drooped, and he was the very picture of a defeated man.

"Are you done yet?" I asked.

"Because really," said Omar, "we need to get going."

Slivers made a face as if he were concentrating hard, began to count on his fingers, shook his head no, put three of the fingers down, began counting again, did a little take where he pretended that he was distracted by his thumb.

"I'm supposed to…now what was it?" He splayed his hands out to the side in the classic, "beats me" pose and made another big, sad clown face.

"WHAT?!" we shouted.

"Ah yes! I'm supposed to take you back. To your time." Slivers stood up and did a little dance of satisfaction, and then bowed.

"You know how to do that, right?"

Slivers' face grew serious. "With every fiber of my being," he said. "Clown's honor." He put his hand to his heart, raised his other hand to his forehead in a military salute, switched the hands, switched them back and then executed a perfect pratfall backwards over the bench.

"Clowns," I muttered.

"I'm okay," he called out from the ground behind the bench.

CHAPTER TWENTY-EIGHT: HOMEWARD BOUND

Slivers stood up and made an elaborate pantomime of brushing off his clothes. "Are you ready?"

"Don't we need to find another Great Wandini?"

"Oh yes, I almost forgot. Now where is it?" He began to walk in tight little circles, looking at the ground as if he expected to find something underfoot.

Omar and I waited and watched for a full minute, and then both shouted at once, "SLIVERS!"

"Oh, right," he muttered. "Follow me."

We walked down the boardwalk, ducked into a building that was empty and vacant, walked out the back door, went through three dark alleys and straight through a dance hall where couples were twirling each other around to the strains of accordion music, and then Slivers stopped at another building with boarded up windows. He tried the door, found it unlocked, and then gestured to us to follow him. It was dark inside, and I thought I heard the sound of rats scurrying. It smelled musty and damp, like it hadn't been open for decades.

"Why can't it ever be in, like, a well-lit normal place?" said Omar. "Why does it always have to be at the very back of the creepiest warehouse imaginable?"

"Beats me," I said. "Maybe this clown is just being dramatic."

"Oh, good one, Josh."

Slivers turned a corner and there it was, The Great Wandini. He was shiny and brand new, the paint fresh and gleaming and the glass dome that encased the magician's head sparkling. He still looked like Vice-President Joe Biden. Weird.

Slivers held his hand out and said, "Tokens, please."

Omar and I reached into our pockets and handed them over.

"Great," said Slivers. "Now give me the tokens."

"We just did."

"No, you didn't."

"You're holding them right there in your hand," shouted Omar.

"No, I'm not."

I gave Omar a look and shook my head and rolled my eyes. I repeat...clowns.

So I held my hand out flat, palm facing up, looked up to the ceiling and said, "Just give me the tokens."

Slivers' face contorted, and he put his hand to his mouth in a gesture of confusion. "No," he said, "YOU just give ME the tokens."

"Just give ME the tokens."

"You give ME the tokens."

"Tokens, please."

"Now just hold your horses…"

"Okay, horses held. Now give ME the tokens."

"I said that first."

"I said that first."

"Gimme it."

"Right. Gimme it."

He bit his lip, confused. "Okay, sure," said Slivers, opening his fist and handing back the tokens.

I took them, rubbed them on my shirt, and handed them back to him. "Thanks," I said. "Now here are the tokens."

He took them from me without another word and slipped them into his pocket. "Don't mention it," he said. "Now where were we?"

"You were sending us back to Oregon in the future," Omar said.

"Absolutely."

I waited. Slivers appeared to be admiring some birds that had settled on a beam near the ceiling. "So send us," Omar said.

"What?"

"Send us. What are you waiting for?"

"Send you where?"

"Send us home!"

"Oh, right. Why didn't you say so?" Slivers slipped the tokens into the machine.

There was a flash of bright, white light, the floor of the old building felt like it was melting under our feet, but I had the odd sensation of not feeling disoriented or like I was falling. I just kind of…floated.

And then my sight came back into focus, my feet felt firmly planted on the ground and I found myself standing beside Slivers' warehouse in downtown McMinnville. My bike was leaned up against the side of the building where I had left it. A homeless guy named Skin stood paralyzed on the other side of the street, staring at me and then trudging off mumbling about how the government was messing with his head.

I have never been so happy in my life to see a dilapidated old warehouse and vacant alley. Because it was in 2012.

But Omar wasn't there. My heart started to sink, wondering what had happened to my friend, but then he came walking around from the back of the building.

"Huh," he said. "It took me about an extra ten seconds to travel through time. That was pretty cool. Let's never do it again."

"Good idea," I said. "Hang on, I want to check something."

I walked back inside the warehouse, which was dark and deserted. I walked all the way to the back, but it was darker and dustier than ever. A window on the back wall was broken, and there was glass on the floor. The Great Wandini was no longer in the place where it had been. I looked on all of the shelves, but it was gone.

In the corner, where the typeset newspaper sat, there was one final message from Slivers. "Nice work, Class Clown. Always be on time." And just as I finished reading it, the whole thing shimmered and vanished.

I went back outside, got on my bike, and began to ride. Omar rode behind me on his bike.

"You'd better get home," he called out. "Your mom thinks you've been camping."

"I hate camping," I yelled over my shoulder.

"I know," he said.

We continued to ride together, but then I remembered something, so I pulled over to the side of the road again. The cars that went by us looked like huge dinosaurs compared to the horse and buggies and old cars to which I had become accustomed in 1908. Everything was a little less green here, smelled a lot better, and felt a hundred percent like home, where I belonged.

I reached inside my shirt and pulled out my grouch bag. "Remember that quarter you gave me? Thought I'd give it back."

I reached inside the bag and felt around. There was a coin in there, but from its size and weight, I knew it wasn't the quarter I had left with. I pulled it out, and with it a scrap of paper. "Thought you wouldn't mind a souvenir from your visit. Thanks for everything, Josh. Your pals, The Marx Brothers."

Speechless for a change, I handed it over to Omar. "Wow," he breathed. It was an 1895 Barber quarter, with Lady Liberty's head in profile on the front under the words In God We Trust. Thirteen stars circled her head, and the year, 1895, was stamped on the bottom. The back said United States of America around an eagle who clutched a branch in one talon and arrows in the other.

"May the Barf be with you," I said. Omar and I always said that to each other. Always will, too. It was a line from the movie Spaceballs.

We later found out that Barber quarters are extremely rare and are worth about $1,437 at present auction rates. But Omar said he wanted to keep it, because what might it be worth in another one-hundred-twenty years?

And what about the 2012 quarter that Chico Marx took from me? Well, it is still worth a quarter, but I'm sure that he won a lot of bets with it in his time.

"Omar, my friend," I said, punching him on the shoulder, "a very wise old man named Groucho once said these immortal words. 'When I came to this town twenty years ago I didn't have a nickel in my pocket. Now I've got a nickel in my pocket.' Or in your case, a quarter that's worth a fortune."

Omar smiled. "Why, that's the most ridiculous thing I've ever heard," he said. "Say the secret word and win a trip to McMinnville, Oregon."

He punched me back. It didn't hurt at all, at least not compared to Daisy's punches. We pedaled together almost all the way to my house before Omar peeled off and went down his street. My mother made stuffed cabbage and told me to put my camping clothes in the wash. I hate stuffed cabbage, but remembering the horrible gruel soup at the Oneida Textile Mills, I ate three helpings. And appreciated every bite of it.

Afterwards, the kids all met at the tennis courts at Patton Middle School, and I told them everything.

They were disappointed. Tough crowd.

They didn't' believe that I had spent nearly a week in 1908 and almost got stuck there forever.

"Wait a minute, didn't you guys all go back into time with The Great Wandini?"

They looked at me like I was nuts.

"No!" they shouted.

I looked at Omar and he just shrugged. Somebody was gonna have a lotta 'splainin to do."

They called me all kinds of names that rhymed with "liar," and threatened great bodily harm if I didn't come up with a better story for why I'd missed all of spring break. That's when Omar pulled out his 1895 quarter and showed everyone, and for once, they all shut up and just gaped.

"Big deal," said Stevie San Pedro. "I've got, like, five old quarters like that at home. That quarter doesn't prove anything. You can buy them off the internet."

I pulled out my grouch bag from under my shirt and told them what it was.

"As if," snorted Stevie. "Like I'm really freaking sure that Groucho Marx gave you a grouch bag. Did Harpo give you a harp?"

When I went back to school on Monday, Mr. Yanuzzi had forgotten all about my detention. I have a certain slivery clown to thank for that.

And later that week, my Dad came down from the attic with a puzzled look on his face. "Josh," he said, "can I have a word with you? Look at what I just found in your grandfather's old box of things. I could swear I've been through that a dozen times since he passed away and I never saw this before."

It was a black-and-white publicity photo of the Marx Brothers from one of their movies. All of my buddies were there: Groucho, Harpo, Chico, Gummo and Zeppo, all grinning at the camera and very much the big, comic movie stars that they deserved to be. Written on the photo in a hand that I recognized as Julius's were these words: "To Josh Markowitz, the Class Clown. With all of our thanks and love. From your pals, the Marx Brothers."

"Now how in the world . . . " my dad started. "This would have been with your grandpa literally years before you were even born. How could they even know your name?"

"Beats me," I said. "Must be one of life's little secrets."

Honk.

I am Josh Markowitz, the Class Clown of Patton Middle School, and that was my story.

Applause. APPLAUSE!! I'd like to thank my mother, and my father, and The Great Wandini, and the Academy, whatever the Academy is. And Slivers, may his spirit continue to inspire future comedians and sundry jokers.

Don't throw flowers, throw money.

Did someone say money?

Well now, I'm all ears.

POSTSCRIPT: FROM THE DIARY OF AMY CONNORS

School is back in session and I am literally grinding my teeth to get through these last days before the end of the year and I can GET OUT of the seventh grade. My teeth are literally like little Chiclets that are almost worn away to nothing because of the grinding, I am so ready for this year to be over. Time . . . passes . . . soooooo . . . .slowly.

Everyone is very disappointed because my cousin Lizzie, the one and only Elizabeth Walcot Woolcott, had to go back to the Kensington neighborhood of London where she lives, and which is very posh. She didn't even say goodbye to me or the other kids at school. She just kind of vanished all of a sudden without even leaving a note or a text or anything. The only thing she left me was a plaid scarf ("not so posh," she wrote on a slip of paper that she stapled to it, "you can have it"), her white go-go boots ("very posh, but my feet have grown in America," she wrote on another note), and a weird old flyer written on cheap paper that says something about a new play being staged at the Globe Theater somewhere in England. The play was called "The Tempest," and the paper has a signature scrawled across the back that looks like "Wm. Shaykspoor" or something.

As if I'm supposed to know who that is.

I kind of miss her, and I felt bad telling Josh Markowitz that she left, because I know that he liked her. He can just get in line. Stevie San Pedro liked her, too, but every time I see him these days he goes all pale and runs away.

It's really okay with me that she left. I mean, we had lots of good times together, and she is my cousin after all. Nearly identical cousin, and all that. Or all of that rot, as Lizzie would have said.

But don't feel bad, dear diary. I just got a message on Facebook from another distant shore that is even more posh, I mean chic, than the Kensington neighborhood of London. This one came straight from Paris and said that my other cousin, Brigitte Brioche, would be arriving soon and please fix up a chambre, I mean room, for her, because she would be staying with us. She will require two croissants and something called Café au Lait every morning, and could Mom please learn how to force-feed a goose, because goose liver is the only thing besides croissants that Brigitte eats.

So toute suite *and* hors d'oeuvres, *dear Diary. Or as dear Lizzie would have said, "Toodle-oo."*

Eighth grade at Patton Middle School is going to be one wild ride.

-- THE END --

About the Author and about GROUCH BAG:

Jim Gullo lives in McMinnville, Oregon with his wife, two sons, a dog named Louis and a rabbit named Fat Boy who is pure dynamite. There really is a Patton Middle School just down the street from his house. There might even be a torture chamber in the basement there, but he's too afraid to find out.

Jim has been a huge fan of the Marx Brothers for as long as he can remember, and it was a total blast for him to imagine and write these scenes of them as young men. This kind of novel, or fiction book, is called a fictionalization, which is a fancy word to describe a made-up book that utilizes real-life people and situations. Most of the historical facts, as well as the personalities of the Marx Brothers, are as close to being accurate as Jim could make them.

The Marx Brothers really did live on East 93rd Street in New York City for a time with their parents, Sam (Frenchie) and Minnie, and Harpo did work for a short time as a bellboy at the Seville Hotel, which still exists, albeit as an Ace Hotel, in downtown Manhattan.

The story of Harpo leaving school because bullies threw him out the window is also true. Here's another nugget about Harpo: He was originally named Adolph, as written in this book, but later changed his name to Arthur until finally, in about 1914, getting his stage name during a poker game. He and his brothers – Groucho, Chico, Harpo, Gummo and Zeppo -- used their stage names for the rest of their lives in both the public and private arenas. They called each other Groucho and Harpo, et cetera. Their wives and friends called them by those names, too.

Before becoming comedians, they really did perform as singers called The Four Nightingales, and played at Henderson's on Coney Island, among many other places.

And, of course, grouch bags were real and were worn by traveling performers to safeguard their valuables. They weren't invented by Julius "Groucho" Marx – it was just a coincidence that his stage name shared the word "grouch" with the bag that he wore around his neck as a young, vaudeville performer.

Some things were changed for the sake of this story, especially the timing of events. Harpo didn't actually learn to play the harp until much later than 1908, and the brothers' conversion to comedy didn't occur for several years afterwards. When it did happen, though, with the brothers ad-libbing and hurling insults at an unruly audience one day, it was magical, and they never went back to being singers. It would take them years of honing their comedy act, but they went from performing on vaudeville to having their own Broadway shows, to movies and even to television. Late in his career, Groucho starred in a very funny quiz show on TV called, "You Bet Your Life."

Jim's favorite Marx Brothers movies are *Duck Soup, A Night at the Opera, A Day at the Races* and *Horsefeathers.* You will see where the African explorer scenario came from if you watch *Animal Crackers*, where Groucho plays a character named Captain Spalding. One of their early Broadway hits, *The Cocoanuts*, is still revived in repertory theaters, and in 2016 there was a revival in New York of the musical revue, *I'll Say She Is*, which was their first big hit on stage, but was lost for decades before Marx historians pieced it together. The Brothers are still hugely popular; there are even Facebook pages devoted to them with hundreds of avid followers who post photos and reminiscences of the Marx Brothers.

If you'd like to learn more about them, Jim recommends Harpo's autobiography, "Harpo Speaks," which gives the family history and great insights into each of the brothers. But the best way to learn about the Marx Brothers is to simply watch and enjoy their movies. They were the gold standard for bright, wise-cracking, satiric comedy, and were true masters of their art.

Many thanks are in order to friends and family who patiently read and offered advice during the writing of this book, which was more than three years in the making and underwent several revisions, as most good books do. They are Christian Schoon, Teresa DiFalco, Steve SanFillipo, Lynne Gullo, Carol Lee, Dave Margolis (who found and sent Jim an article about the real Slivers the Clown), Jon Pult (who wrote the Slivers article for clownalley.blogspot.com), Noah Diamond (who is a real Groucho impersonator and Marx Bros. historian in New York City), Clete Barrett Smith, Girl Friday Productions, and Leslie Ann Miller. Kris Gullo, Joe Gullo, Michael Gullo and Henry Gullo deserve special recognition for reasons that will be entirely clear to them.

Sam Gladstein, to whom this book is dedicated, was a warm and funny man with a great twinkle in his eye who looked a little bit like a Marx Brother, and who will always be remembered with affection. He lived just long enough to see an early version of the book that was dedicated to him.

Thanks for reading GROUCH BAG. Keep laughing, stay cheerful, and if you ever get confused by life, order another hard-boiled egg.

My e-mail address is jim (at) jimgullo.com. Send me your favorite Marx Brothers story or line or tell me what you like or didn't like about the book.

And now, in conclusion, I will offer this:
A very famous pig who I admired very much
once said this, and now, so shall I:

A thee, a thee, a thee, uh…that's all, folks.

– Jim Gullo
McMinnville, Oregon
November 2016